BONNE VIE IN PROVENCE

A Travel Guide for the Soul

GEORGIE GROSSMAN

- First edition, 2025
- Second printing, 2026

ISBN: 979-8-9937125-0-5

Cover Design and Interior Layout: Ronda Taylor, HeartworkCreative.com

Better Books Publishing House
Dallas, TX
Betterbookspub.com

Contents

Magic Calls

From a spit of land in a bend of the Rhône River, Bonne Vie calls.

Come! Feel my magic. Let me flow through you.

Over the years, lives have been changed, and tales have been told, but as our story begins, the villa stands empty, waiting. Waiting for someone to heed its call. Someone whose heart is open and willing to share Bonne Vie's gift.

Bonne Vie

Some may think that I am the stone that forms the walls of this house, that I am the wood of the rafters and the tile of the roof that shields those within. But I am not this house. I abide within this dwelling as I have from the day the dream of home was conceived.

I was here when the Romans claimed this land.

I filled their grapes with promise and their olives with liquid gold, just as I do today.

I flow through the roots of trees and upward through outstretched limbs that yearn to touch the sky.

I ripen apricots with the rosy hues of the sun, a promise of more summers to come.

I play among the falling water of fountains, stirring joy in the hearts of those who recognize my dance.

I float between the notes of bird song at dawn as each new day is revealed.

I have been claimed by many, but appreciated by few, for gratitude has always been essential for unlocking my legacy.

I fill the hearts of those who invite me in, those who wish for peace and look for joy.

I fill the hearts of those with great dreams and those who dream of nothing more than peace.

Madame and Monsieur's love was a lens that drew me from the earth and amplified my power. After Madame's death, that lens lay dormant, my energy but embers carried within the people whose lives it had touched.

Today, I am again called from the earth, focused by the joy of Bonne Vie's newest residents. Their light shines, telling the world that the magic of this place has not been lost.

Drink from my fountain. I am here for all who will receive me.

I am Bonne Vie.

I am love.

1

L'Enchanteur

Le Chat, April 2011

THE CRUNCH OF GRAVEL UNDER THE WEIGHT OF HEAVY TIRES WAKES me. Warm morning sunshine, a light breeze, and the smell of lavender are what I expect from my morning nap, not the disturbing crunch of gravel. But this morning, my sleep has been interrupted by a truck lumbering up my driveway. From my patch of sunshine on the patio, I see two men jump down from the cab and stretch from what I can only assume has been a long ride. The driver pulls a phone out of his pocket and chats lazily to the beautiful woman at the other end of the call. You can always tell when a man is talking to a beautiful woman; his body softens, and his smile broadens.

Seems these guys have a wait ahead of them, as they've lit their cigarettes and wandered into the garden. Ah, my garden. It was once finely manicured, filled with a riot of color from April through September. The color remains, and the bees float from petal to petal, but the crisp lines have faded into a mixture of weeds and overgrown design. How I miss the way the sunflowers stood tall in their beds, outlined by smartly groomed paths of gravel. And I miss the look of the cosmos, with their frilly leaves fluttering in the breeze, and the rosemary perfuming the air each time I brushed past it while making my daily inspection.

It's been a while since anyone has cared for my garden. I've lost track of how long it's been since someone has bent to pull a weed or rake the gravel to restore order to that which nature has unraveled. Though the *jardinier* no longer tends to my garden, he does stop by every so often to share his lunch and check to see that the water drips into my bowl. I knew he was a good man the first day I wandered through the gates of Bonne Vie.

I stretch in the sun, pulling my claws across the patio tiles as I prepare to move to a higher vantage point. From experience, I know that seeing men in trucks means more people will soon be coming or going. To the wall, over the branch, and onto the roof I move, settling in dappled sunlight.

Not long after I'm settled, and before I can fall back to sleep, a car comes bouncing down the driveway. That dip in the path always catches those in a hurry. There used to be a sign on the gate to prevent that, but it disappeared last year with some tourists.

The car comes to a stop, doors fly open, and out pop four people— all babbling at once.

"What a great place to put a pool!"

The splashing of the fountain is quite enough water for me, thank you.

"Can you believe the size of those trees?"

That's why Madame called them her centurions.

"I can see a canopy over the patio."

Oh, please, that will ruin my morning sunbathing.

"My flower garden would be perfect there!"

We have a garden. It just needs to have its edges straightened.

Please, Lord, let these people make a quick once-around the place and leave like the other tourists who have stumbled through the gates over the past few years.

My two friends from the truck come around the house, and everyone does the obligatory meet-and-greet, French style. When the hugs and kisses are finished, the woman runs back to the car, rummages around, and returns with a key. Cheering, the small crowd heads to the door. After fumbling with the lock, they excitedly tumble through the door, leaving it open behind them. Looks like it's time for a change of perspective. I haven't seen the inside of the house at floor level in ages.

Hey, this place doesn't look bad. A little dusty, but not bad. The sun still shines through the kitchen window, though that rose bush could use a trim. The large kitchen counter, which in days gone by was set with bowls of fruit and vegetables, and pies to cool, sprawls across the center of the room. The double doors from the solarium to the back patio have a few cracked panes of glass ... must be from that strong Mistral earlier this spring when the plane tree branch crashed across the yard.

The sprawling living room lays wide open as the furniture has been pushed into a corner, but most of it is still here: the couch, the coffee table, the end table, the two tall-backed chairs that used to sit in front of the fireplace, assorted lamps .... Hmm, where's my favorite chair? The big overstuffed one that everyone fought to sit in, when I wasn't in it. It must be here, somewhere under this sheet.

I hear banging in the basement. I hope they've left the door open. Musty, as usual. Here, in the dust of the storeroom, the shelves are empty except for a few forgotten jars someone pushed into the shadows years ago. The wine cellar door is closed. I wonder if those special bottles of wine Madame had hidden away are still there.

There's a lot of excited discussion going on in the back room. What is it about that old furnace that people find so interesting? All that matters is the warm air that floats through the floor grates when the sun's rays are no longer enough to heat the floor tiles. Who cares if it belches and gurgles? The sounds just remind us that our house is alive.

Here they come, I'd better get upstairs before they do. I remember the last time I got stuck in the basement. Everyone was mad at me, but it wasn't my fault they didn't hear me meowing until after midnight.

I wonder how things are upstairs. Yep, just as I remember, six rooms, four of them with grand beds, chairs, dressing tables, and armoires. Hope the window seat on the west side still catches the setting sun. Monsieur's easy chair was always a great place for my early evening naps. And the east bedroom, I've always loved its double French doors that open onto the upper balcony. I remember the nights I'd slip through the open balcony doors and hop into bed with Madame. She never complained about my purring, just pulled me close and snuggled up.

There's a ruckus in the front yard. What are they up to now?

Slipping out between the open door and jamb, I find all six of the visitors huddled at the truck, making plans to unload and distribute its contents. I'm not sure how I feel about this. It would be nice to have someone open doors for me again and tend to my garden, but I fear my naps will be disturbed.

Times do change, and I sense a new beginning for the villa.

Could it be that love has returned?

2

Second Act

WENDY, APRIL 2011

MY LEG IS SHAKING! I MUST BE MORE EXHAUSTED THAN I THOUGHT. Through closed eyes, I can tell the sun is up, but my lids are too heavy to open. Yesterday's excitement left me drained. I float off again.

There's that vibration again. It's getting stronger. What did I do to my leg? Stretching, my leg presses against a weight on top of the sheet. It's not Dave, I can hear him breathing on the other side of me.

Sunlight rushes in as I open my eyes just a crack. It's a cat! A cat is sleeping next to me! And just beyond, the terrace door stands ajar. Closing my eyes again, I float off in thought. Did I leave the door open last night? I remember listening to the sounds of the night from the balcony before collapsing into bed. I thought I'd shut it.

"Hello, kitty! What's your name?" Stretching my hand down to the lump at my knee, I give a little scratch, and the vibration increases. My entire left side begins to shake, and I sink back into the bed, allowing my senses to take in my surroundings: a cacophony of bird calls, the scent of lavender and jasmine carried on the softly rattling breeze that fills the open door.

We are in France! We are in Provence! And it's not just a vacation. This is home now. We are living a fairy tale. I can't believe we did this!

Sometimes, unexpected endings are gifts in disguise. Last May, Dave was "offered" a retirement package he couldn't turn down. Over a celebratory bottle of champagne, we decided it was time to live life to the fullest. We were ready for adventure.

The following Monday, I told my principal I was retiring and would be using my sick leave days to cover the remainder of the school year. After a week of tearful goodbyes, I began the job of organizing our bucket list and packing for a three-month stay in a B&B outside of Avignon.

And so it was. We began our retirement with a romp through the Côtes du Rhône, blissfully indulging in the best that southern France had to offer. We had spent years savoring French wine from Dave's collection and enjoying the French cuisine we had learned to prepare from Jacques and Julia, while dreaming of Provence. Lesson number one: There is no comparison. **Real life is better than the dream.**

From our *gîte* in Orange, not far from Avignon, we took day trips to Mt. Ventoux, to Montpellier and Sète on the coast, and Nîmes to the west. We spent days hiking through vineyards into the trees and beyond into the Dentelles, the small chain of mountains that run through the Department of Vaucluse. Oh, and the nights of sitting under the stars, being part of the dinner scene in tiny Caderousse, where a once Michelin-starred chef chooses to serve excellent meals to friends, neighbors, and tourists who are lucky enough to wander upon his establishment. Dinners there are like a play with the characters filtering in over an hour's time - couples, singles, families with young children, teenagers, and whoever else makes the playlist each night. There is only one seating and everyone is expected to play their part—the happy birthday boy, the bride-to-be celebrating her upcoming nuptials, lovers sharing a romantic meal, and grandchildren entertaining their grandparents. Doing our part on that night, we were the retirees who made a wish for the play to never end.

And then came the day our wish was granted.

The sun warmed my face as I leaned towards the open window to let the breeze blow over me. We had been wandering the narrow roads of the countryside with no destination in mind. That morning, we bought bread, cheese, fruit, and a bottle of wine at the farmers' market. Grabbing a brightly colored blanket from our *gîte,* we jumped into the car and set off to explore the country roads.

Passing through fields of lavender, rows of sunflowers with their heads following the sun's path, and sand-colored country homes, their windows framed with bright blue shutters, I felt at peace.

As we meandered along, I was pulled towards an opening in a tall stone wall. "Slow down. I want to check this place out."

Dave slowed to a creep as I leaned further out the window to take in the high wall with the vines peaking over the top.

"Stop! I want to look in." I struggled to see down the drive, as the sweeping branches of willow and tall weeds filled the yard. "Let's go in!"

"What if some old couple is living there and they call the police? How we bailed ourselves out of a French jail is NOT part of the vacation story I want to tell our friends." Dave has always been one to follow rules.

"Quit thinking the worst. If someone asks, we'll tell them we're lost and looking for directions. Something about this place tells me if we don't go in, we'll always wonder what we missed."

As usual, my curiosity overcame Dave's worries, and the thought of a new adventure drew us up the winding drive. Halfway in, we hit a dip that made our heads bounce against the roof. Dave brought the car to a crawl. Creeping towards the house, we realized we were in a world that called for a slower pace and a different state of being.

At one time, the grounds around this house, this mansion, had been beautifully designed and well groomed. Fruit and nut trees cast small patches of shade, and the leaves of the olive trees shimmered in the breeze. From this side of the wall, we could see the gnarled grape vines that peeked at me over the top. Gravel paths outlined a now wildly overgrown garden. Butterflies fluttered in a breeze that carried the call of birds. Closing my eyes, I imagined the sound of falling water in a fountain now gone dry. From our cursory exploration of the place, we could tell no one had lived there for quite a while. Sadly, that meant no one had appreciated the garden either. It only seemed appropriate that we did.

"This is the perfect place for our picnic."

Dave pulled the food from the back seat as I spread the blanket on a flat area near the back door. The bright red and white pattern of the blanket set a place from which to enjoy the wild beauty of "our" garden as we feasted.

After lunch, we lay on our backs watching the leaves of the olive trees flit from silver to green and back again. I lazily floated in and out of a dreamy state of contentment. Questions wandered through my mind. Who created this lovely oasis? Why has it been abandoned?

Reluctantly, we packed away our lunch basket and drove towards the road. We had to know the story of this place. When we got to the gate, we noticed a sign hanging askew. It said:

Laissez le monde derrière vous, ralentissez et profitez de la vie.

Dave was sure someone in town would be able to help us read the sign and learn more about the house, so he carefully unhooked the one place where the sign was still attached and laid it on the back seat before we reluctantly turned out of the gate. "Once we've decoded the sign's message, we'll go by the *Bricolage* and find the right hooks to reattach it to the gate. A place this beautiful should be suitably adorned."

Stopping at the café in town, we contemplated the sign. As we settled into a table near the street, Dave waved at the owner just inside the door.

"*Bonjour! Deux cafés, s'il vous plaît*" Dave loves to practice his French. Unfortunately, being able to greet people and place an order in a café wasn't helping us understand the sign before us.

When the owner arrived, he almost spilled our espressos. Seeing the sign on the table, he slammed down our cups and stalked off, red-faced, fists clenched, as though he was about to explode.

"What's up with him?"

"I think it has something to do with the sign. He was fine until he saw it. I wonder what it says."

"The only words I can make out are *le monde* and *la vie*—the world and the life."

"You know, *la Poste* seems to have a lot of services here in France. I mean, where else do you find a bank in a post office? Maybe they could help us. They had to deliver mail to the villa when whoever lived there was around."

We picked up the sign, and Dave left a 5-euro note on the table, as our host was nowhere to be found.

The reaction of the staff at *la Poste* wasn't much better. Their eyes wide as if insulted, the two women behind the counter carried on a heated dialogue before one of them abruptly said *"Allez à la banque,"* and pointed across the square. Dave nodded and backed away from the counter.

"Maybe we should forget this whole thing. Whatever this sign says, it makes people angry."

"Maybe we're just running into that French attitude we've heard about. Let's try the bank. If they can't help, we'll wait and ask Julia back at the *gîte*."

"I hear there's a new computer program coming out that can translate languages into English."

"That would be nice, but right now we don't have a computer, so we're going to have to depend on people."

Walking through L'Esprit du Rhône, we admired the quaint buildings surrounding the square with a fountain in the middle and trees lining the walks. The wider main street splits to create a roundabout at the square and then merges once more to run out the other side of town. Narrower streets radiate from the center. The bank and the *mairie*, town hall, are on the opposite end of the square from *la Poste*, while the café sits on one side. Not wanting to draw the café owner's ire, we chose to walk on the far side of the fountain, where we passed a *boulangerie* and *boucherie*. What a lovely town with all of the necessary institutions that make living in France a delight.

The bank, a large, dark edifice, was more than just a location for distributing money; it was a symbol of stability and security. We could tell this old building had been the center of the town's economic life since its inception. In reverence, we walked into the cavernous hall lit by a grand chandelier. High marble counters housed tellers, and on either side of the main hall were doors to offices, each with a large dark desk and a matching high-backed chair, while two seats were arranged before the desk from which occupants could solicit the bank's assistance.

Maybe because we were standing in awe or because we were blocking the door, someone finally approached us.

"Bonjour, puis-je vous aider?"

"Parlez-vous anglais?"

Raising a finger, the young man turned and spoke to his associate, who disappeared into one of the offices near the tellers' counter and returned with a gentleman whose bearing announced that he was in charge.

"Good day, I am Louis De La Cour. How may I help you?"

Taking the sign from Dave's hand, I held it up. "We would like to know what this sign says and to know about the estate where it was hanging. The ladies at *la Poste* directed us to your bank."

Again, that look of horror. Now the entire staff was looking at us as though we had announced a robbery. The gentleman quickly recovered his composure and invited us into his office, while the faces of the staff turned away as we passed.

"I think your curiosity may have gotten us in real trouble this time, Wendy. Is anyone on the phone making a call to the *gendarmerie*?" I nudged Dave with my elbow and quietly prayed that he was wrong.

As we settled into large, overstuffed chairs, I placed the sign on the ornate wooden desk and stammered, "We didn't mean to cause any problems, we're just curious about what the sign says and who owns the beautiful old estate. It seems such a waste to have it be sitting there unappreciated."

Sadness filled M. De La Cour's eyes. "Yes, it is a shame to see Bonne Vie empty."

"So, someone does own it."

"I am sorry to say that the bank has owned the estate since Madame's death four years ago." M. De La Cour's eyes clouded over as though lost in a memory.

"Is it for sale? There was no real estate sign."

Dave and I looked at each other. Were we thinking the same thing?

"With the crash in 2008, interest in the estate disappeared. It was decided to remove the sign. We didn't want to invite unsavory visitors."

"I promise we're not unsavory, and we adore the house and grounds. But why does everyone look at us as though we have the plague when they see this sign? What does it say?"

M. De La Cour gave a little laugh. "That was Monsieur's doing. After the truck delivering the furnace churned a hole in the drive, Monsieur decided not to fill it. He wanted visitors to slow down, not just their driving, but their minds as well. He added the sign as a warning. It says,

Leave the world behind, enjoy life."

Dave and I smiled, remembering the jarring bounce as we drove in. We nodded in understanding.

"But why is everyone so outraged when they see the sign? The French are all about *joie de vivre*."

"It's not the words. That sign has hung on the gate of Bonne Vie for as long as anyone can remember. We all know who it belongs to. You have removed a part of the town's memory."

Dave handed the sign to M. De La Cour. "Please have it returned and securely hung on the gate."

M. De La Cour took the sign with a bow of the head as though he were receiving a communion wafer.

Almost in unison, Dave and I asked, "How much does the bank want for the property?"

An hour later, we left the bank, signed *promesse de vente* in hand. We had ten days to visit the property and finalize our decision. Like children with a new toy, we dreamt of where life would take us.

M. De La Cour had arranged for someone to meet us at the house in the morning. That night, when we dined in our favorite restaurant in Caderousse, we were the couple for whom the dream was beginning.

The next step was to employ a *notaire* who spoke English. We didn't have far to go as the town *notaire* occupied the office next to the bank. Madame Bonheur, *notaire* at the signing of the *promesse de vente*, spoke English, was familiar with the property, and, most importantly, was happy to work with two Americans who had no idea how to navigate the French *marché immobilier*.

Dave exploded, "8%! I'll never complain about realtor fees in the US again."

We quickly learned why Madame Bonheur's fee was 8%. She would act much like a Title Company in the US, but when people tell you there's a lot of paperwork involved in buying property in France, they mean serious paperwork. At first, Dave insisted on knowing what every paper said—the list of required forms filled two pages in his travel journal. After spending the day translating and trying to understand one form, Dave decided he would trust Madame Bonheur to do her job.

The rest of our holiday was spent learning about the French real estate process, negotiating a price, and planning our transition from tourists to residents of France. Since the estate had been vacant for so long and required significant renovation, we were able to negotiate a reasonable price. And since we'd discovered the property and found our way to his office on our own, M. De La Cour decided to forgo the estate agent's fee, making our dream an even more affordable investment.

Yes, investment, and that's where Lee and Josh came in.

Returning to the States filled with excitement, we shared our story with friends who were sure we had left our brains at the bottom of an empty bottle of Châteauneuf-du-Pape: everyone, but Lee and Josh.

As longtime international travelers, they understood our joy and showered us with questions as we considered just what we would do with our new home.

Years before, Dave had responded to an emergency plea for help. It was a Saturday morning during the first fall cold snap, and Lee had lost a large filling from one of his molars. Seems his partner, Josh, had taken the cold weather as a sign to bake. And bake he did -extra gooey sweet rolls, the caramel of which latched on to Lee's already loose filling, leaving him with a gapingly painful hole. Being the foodie that he is, Dave agreed to a weekend repair if Lee would bring a sample of the gooey culprit with him. By the time the repair was complete, the guys realized they not only loved Josh's sweet rolls, but they also shared a love of French food and French wine. Lee's stories of graduate school in France and Dave's love of French wine and food were the beginning of a beautiful friendship that quickly brought the four of us together.

Lee, the architect, asked, "What type of architecture does this villa of yours have?"

"You tell us! Let me grab my laptop, and we'll give you a tour."

Ten minutes later, the four of us were watching a video of me narrating a tour through the house and garden. Was that only a month ago? I felt like I was watching a different person in a different era.

As we watched the "French" me wave goodbye on the screen, Lee's eyes were glistening. "That's quite a house. What are you going to do with all that space?"

"Host all of the people who come to visit, of course."

"Looks like you've got a lot of work ahead of you. You may want to consider a way to recoup your expenses, maybe a Bed and Breakfast?"

"Hmm, I've heard being a B&B host takes quite a bit of work. Besides, we'd like to travel too."

"Maybe what you need are partners." Lee gave Josh that *'go with me on this'* look.

Josh jumped in, "You'll need a chef and someone to write text for the website."

An interior designer and a chef/writer on the team, how could we go wrong?

By the time we finished sharing photos of the town and the surrounding countryside, Lee and Josh were entirely on board. It was that night, over an exquisite bottle of *Vin de Pays,* that our plan to join forces and turn the *maison* into a bed and breakfast was born. Lee & Josh's investment in the villa would free up funds to update the property and create a joint business that would allow both couples to enjoy life in a small French village and have the flexibility to travel.

Saying goodbye to our life in Virginia was more difficult than you may think, even though we knew we were walking into a dream. The big decision to move to France ended up being easier than the weight of the many smaller decisions that followed. How many pairs of heels would I wear in my new life? Was shipping my dishes and glassware worth the cost? Should I take my mother's Hummel figurines only to have them shipped back to my niece when I die? And the junk drawer, I didn't even look. Years of rubber bands, twist ties, keys from long-forgotten doors, souvenir magnets that had lost their magnets, and the cheap tape measure, not in metric units, all went into the garbage. At the end of each day, I would collapse from the emotional exhaustion of making decisions and letting go of things.

Sitting before my library of cookbooks, I cried. My collection of well over a hundred books had to be culled. We decided to ship some of our kitchenware and personal belongings, but the furniture, *sans* Dave's favorite chair and my old hope chest, would not be joining us in France, and neither would most of our books. Ultimately, we each chose our favorite fifty books. Dave spent weeks shifting books from one pile to another as he decided what to sell, what to give away, and what to take with him. Now it was my turn. Why had I waited so long?

My **take to France** pile waxed and waned as I relived culinary escapades. Lovingly, I held each book to my chest, reliving the delights each had taken us on. *Basics of Japanese Cooking* took me on a quest for the perfect dashi. That year, I learned to make all six types of dashi and how to use each one. *Mexican Cooking Made Easy* made my mouth water as I remembered the stacks of both flour and corn tortillas that we ate that summer. I laughed 'til I cried when my friend's family recipe for biryani fell from the Indian cookbook. I had not listened to Lakshme's warning to cut back on the chilis in her mother's recipe. Luckily, I had made lots of riata, the cool yogurt and cucumber dish, that helped us survive the ensuing gastric distress. And Julia's *Mastering the Art of French Cooking;* of course, it would go with us. I laughed to myself as I thought of how my new French friends would react to my needing a book to tell me how to make dishes they had absorbed from their mothers.

The most joyful decision was what to do with Dave's wine collection. Shipping the bottles to France would be like taking coals to Newcastle. Instead, a bottle of French wine became our calling card. A trip to the doctor, a bottle of *Châteauneuf-du-Pape.* The mechanic, a nice *Bordeaux.* By the time we left, Allison, my hairdresser, had herself a nice collection of whites from Alsace, and both the Loire and Rhône Valleys. The last bottle I took to her was a *Pouilly-Fuissé* from a north-eastern region near Lyon, with which we toasted to my new life.

"Oh, this one's from a new region. I need to find another pin for my map of France. Wendy, I'm going to miss you and my French wine adventures."

"You know, when you're ready to try the *elusive Châteauneuf-du-Pape Blanc,* you've got a place to stay.

In our wake, we left joyful seeds for the future. Saying goodbye to people became an invitation to share our joy. With every bottle of wine we gave away went a sincere hope that the recipient would visit our new home. We knew that once they walked the fields of lavender and watched the olive leaves flutter in the wind while sitting next to our fountain, the enchantment of Provence would capture their hearts, too.

As for family, we may have to set aside rooms with their names on them.

Though both of us have lost our parents, our relationship with my sister Susan and her husband Mark is quite close. When they had

Megan and Greg, we were joyous. Not being able to have children of our own, we spent 30 years co-parenting their kids. We were there for the skinned knees, lost teeth, high school graduations, and college applications. We share their parents' pride in the accomplished adults Megan and Greg have become. Instead of feeling a loss from our move to France, all four of them are excited to see us widen our horizons and *their* travel opportunities.

Megan peppered me with questions. "How long is the drive from your villa to the beach, Aunt Wendy? You are going to buy one of those cute little Fiats, aren't you? One with a convertible would be a dream."

"You'll have to talk to Dave about the car. They have cars in Europe that you can't find in the United States. Dave is loving his research. He's like a kid in a candy shop. Megan, you know they have topless bathing on the beaches there."

As her mother scowled, Megan squealed with joy. "I'll only need half a bikini!"

"How about mountains? Megan may want to bake on the beach, but I've read there's great climbing in the Alps." Greg, the athlete, had other plans.

"Chamonix is about four hours by car, or you could hop on a train and be there in six. Taking the train saves on the cost of parking once you get there."

Susan looked up from the box she was packing. "You kids can run all over the countryside, but your dad and I are going no further than *Châteauneuf-du-Pape*. I understand there are enough wineries there to keep us busy for quite some time."

And then the decision-making, packing, and planning were completed. There was nothing left to do but get on the plane. Two days ago, we flew out of JFK with two large suitcases. The household items we think will be useful in our new life, and a few touchstones from our past, had been sent ahead. Though we carried very little in our bags, our hearts were brimming with dreams of the future.

Last spring, we were retirees who made a wish for the play to never end. And now, act two has begun.

3

An Affair with French Architecture

Lee, November 2010

WIND BUFFETS THE CAR AS DARK CLOUDS SCUTTLE ACROSS THE sky. It's only November, but it feels like February. Josh and I didn't pack for this cold, so we're wearing half of the clothes from our suitcase just to be warm enough to jump in and out of the car. Having closed on the house last month, Josh and I are here to create a list of tasks that must be completed before the four of us can move in, as well as a list of items that can wait until we are settled. Making the lists won't be the problem. The challenge will be for everyone to agree on what goes on which list.

Earlier this morning, we met with the *agent immobilier* in L'Esprit du Rhône to pick up the keys and get directions to *Bonne Vie*. We knew we were one step closer to being residents of Provence when he gave us the directions.

Go south out of town, turn right at the first house with the blue shutters, cross the bridge, and then drive through the tunnel of plane trees that line the road. Just around the bend to the left, the wall of the property will begin. Turn in at the gate. Beware the dip halfway in!

"Slow down," Dave told us about the dip, and so did the *agent immobilier.*

I take the dip slowly and creep towards the door.

"We're here," Josh whispers in reverence.

"What happened to the wind?"

It's as though the gods are holding it at bay outside the walls.

"You ready for this?" I reach out and squeeze Josh's hand before pushing open the car door. Standing before the century-old doors, I take a deep breath. Amazingly, the old key smoothly flips the latch, and we step over the threshold. Motionless, I take in the entry hall and know that I am home, the home my soul has longed for.

My love affair with French design began my junior year of college when I studied art history in Lyon. Let's face it, when it comes to art, there is no place better to study than France. The French have an innate sense of style, evident in their dress, their cuisine, and the design of their buildings. Whether it be the flamboyant High Gothic or the playfulness of the Rococo period, or even the Neoclassic return to order, for the French, style and design are as much a part of life as good food. It's in their DNA.

Throughout my career as a designer, I struggled to bring that *je ne sais quoi* to my projects. Despite my efforts, I found myself thwarted by clients who couldn't seem to grasp that French design and style extend beyond Louis XIV's ornate gilded furniture and mirror frames.

On this frigid November day, I find myself in the house I have dreamt of since Lyon. This house was built in the early 1850s before the architectural wave of the Second Empire, the style that brought light to the streets of Paris. The villa was originally the home of a wealthy landowner, so its style is much grander than that of a country *manor*, but not as large or grand as a *château*.

As Josh and I stand in the entry, we can see a small sitting area to the left and a larger living area to the right. Our eyes are drawn up the stairs that climb the right side of the entry hall and curve out of sight, leaving us to wonder what lies above. Suspended from the ceiling is a large chandelier cloaked in years of dust and spider webs. With the heavy doors closed behind us, only the sound of our breathing can be heard.

Breaking the silence, I remind Josh. "We're on the ground floor." Pointing up the stairs, "Up there is the first floor."

"Then let's see what this ground floor has to offer." Josh steps to the left, and we begin our exploration. What we thought was a sitting room turns out to be an office. The large, heavy desk, positioned before the high front window, and the shelves that line the walls, tell a story of quiet power.

"I wonder what business deals were made here."

"I can't imagine tearing myself from the view long enough to consider business."

Passing through a set of double doors, we enter the dining room, decorated in Art Deco fashion. Surrounding a broad amboyna burl wood table are a dozen two-tone mohair chairs. Stretching across the wall opposite the windows sits a matching buffet veiled in years of dust. But on this bone-chilling day, it is the massive fireplace that draws our attention.

"A large crackling fire would be wonderful right now."

"Not to mention a bubbly *garbure*. I wonder if there's a chestnut tree on the property. The nuts give the stew a distinct flavor."

"Looks like there's plenty of space to share with friends," I nod towards the table.

We stand lost in our dreams for the room while the light from the windows flanking the fireplace projects our shadows onto the wall.

"Let's see this kitchen I'll be cooking in." Josh pushes through a swinging door on the back wall.

Staring up at the shelves lining the butler's pantry, Josh announces: "Well, that answers the question of where to store the dishes Wendy and I want to bring."

I open one of the dusty drawers, "and both sets of silverware too."

Not knowing what to expect in the kitchen, we nervously leave the butler's pantry and step into an ample, airy space fit for a three-star Michelin chef.

"It, it's wonderful!" Josh sweeps his hand across the heavy wooden work counter that commands the middle of the room. The original stone fireplace on the outer wall is juxtaposed with a stainless-steel sink and a restaurant-sized cooler. We stand with our mouths agape. Josh spies the La Cornue gas stove and almost skips to it. The little boy in him can't resist opening doors and turning knobs. Although dusty, the stove is impeccably free of grease. It was well-maintained over the years.

"I'm almost sure it still works. But I can't be sure until we get the gas reconnected."

While Josh has his head in the oven, I wander about the room. Beyond the kitchen's outer wall, I spy a small prep room that houses an old stone sink and counter, situated below a window that looks out onto an overgrown herb garden, with gnarly old sage and overgrown stubby rosemary bushes.

Only after I promise Josh that he can return to the kitchen before we leave does he follow me to the next room. Through windows covered with years of grime flows a fantastic amount of light. Even on this cloudy day, we watch as motes of dust dance around us like newly awakened fairies, curious about the giants who have disturbed their sleep. Thanks to the thoughtful orientation of the building and the distribution of deciduous trees, sunlight warms the room during these colder months. Leaves that return in the spring will surely provide shade throughout the warmer months, a perfect arrangement for a provincial solarium.

Across the room, a narrower set of doors leads to a small sitting area beneath a porch on this side of the house, balancing the old stone kitchen on the other. The solarium flows into a spacious room that extends to the windows facing the drive. A majestic fireplace spans the outer wall, the stone of the gently curved corbels framing the matching surrounds and supporting a wide marble mantel. Its stately presence creates an air of dignity without being stuffy. With the furniture pushed against the inner wall, I imagine the sounds of a waltz, and the space serving as a ballroom, with dancers gracefully sweeping across the floor.

Back in the entry hall, we allow ourselves to be drawn up the stairs and around the corner, alighting in a well-lit lounge. The ghost of the carpet that had lain in this space for years outlines a cheery sitting area. Surrounding the carpet-less sitting area are well-worn wooden pathways that lead to six doors. Behind the two doors at the front of the house, we find guest rooms overlooking the gravel drive. The two center doors lead to the first chamber of his and her suites, each connected to bedrooms at the rear of the house. The center room on the west side, a lonely library with walls lined by empty bookshelves, is connected to a bedroom via double glass doors. On the east side, a woman's sitting room leads to an understated boudoir. The fireplace, which once provided heat to the room, now stands as a decorative homage to the past, above which a Rococo-era mirror reflects the fascination on our faces.

From each of the rear bedrooms, we can see the winter spoils of a garden and a bit of the fields that lie beyond. Built over the prep kitchen on the west side and the small porch off the solarium on the east are small balconies with French doors from each bedroom.

As is common in French homes even today, there is only one bathroom. What had originally been a separate toilet and bathing area had been united to create one relatively spacious bathroom between the two rear bedrooms. Josh laughs and shakes his head.

"I know what's at the top of the remodeling list." I nod in agreement, scribbling notes in my notebook.

Wandering from room to room, we imagine the stories that unfolded in each space over the years. What important guests may have stayed in the front rooms? What ideas had come to life in the library, and how many parties were dressed for in the sitting rooms? Had Madame and Monsieur taken afternoon tea in the lounge as they planned future soirées?

Among the papers Wendy and Dave had brought back to Virginia was the provenance for the villa. Although it was built in the mid-1800s, the house as we see it today is the result of the previous owners' work. The estate had been remodeled in 1929 when Monsieur Chalon-Arlay purchased the villa as a wedding gift for his young bride.

A home that they shared until he died in the eighties, and where Madame had continued to live until her death a few years ago. Surrounded by these walls, I can feel their love.

Along the back hall between the stairs and the bathroom, we find a door that leads to a hidden staircase, running up to the second floor, and another that leads down to the ground floor. With no natural light, we use our phones to illuminate our path. Modern-day torches in hand, we creep up the narrow staircase, imagining the servants who had once lived here.

At the top of the stairs, we are met by a rusty hinged door that squeals as my shoulder pushes it open. We step into a large living area dimly lit by the sunlight that sneaks in around the closed shutters, giving us glimpses of dust fairies that have followed us on our journey. On the right wall, a sooty fireplace stands as a quiet sentinel. Here at the top of the house, we listen to the rustling of the trees as the cold seeps through our clothes. Behind the doors that line the walls are four small bedrooms, a toilet room, and a cramped bathing area. We stand imagining the life that had filled this cramped space in the few hours the staff had to themselves.

Later, we learn from the realtor that the second floor and the servants' quarters were closed in the late 90s when Madame became ill and no longer entertained.

Carefully making our way back down the steps, we emerge in a small storage room situated behind the entry hall. Another set of stairs leads from the storage room to the basement. Descending the basement stairs, we feel cool, dank air rise around us. Below the kitchen lives an old dragon of a furnace. At one time, this beast had been state-of-the-art and installed to provide warmth more reliably and consistently than the original network of fireplaces. Whether his fiery breath can be reignited and cleanly delivered to the floors above is yet to be discovered.

Adding "French furnace specialist" to my growing list, my stomach knots. What have we gotten ourselves into? Josh snaps a few photos, being sure to get a close-up of the furnace's nameplate before we leave the sleeping monster in its lair.

Murky light filters through the small windows of the cellar. Besides the dragon's lair, there are three other rooms, the largest of them at the foot of the stairs. A wide opening leads into a second room. Shelves embellished with a curious pattern of circles line the walls.

"Jars!" chirps Josh. "This was where they kept the food they canned. What a perfect location, against the walls where the soil can keep them cool all year long."

Happy with himself, Josh hums under his breath and leads the way to the third room, accessible only after another shoulder-wrenching battle with yet another set of rusty hinges. More shelves, but even I know what these are for -- wine! Josh's humming grows louder as he slowly turns, mentally calculating the number of bottles he and Dave can collect.

"We'd better leave before you've spent my entire remodeling budget on a wine collection," I finally mutter.

Leaving Josh to a deeper kitchen inspection, I walk off the size of each room, carefully recording the numbers in my notebook. Thank goodness the wooden floors are in good condition because the cost of rugs would be extreme. I will have to create a spreadsheet of the spaces and their sizes so we can compare them to the Persian rugs we own, as well as the ones Wendy and Dave have. As my remodeling list grows, I am increasingly confident that there will be no budget for new carpets.

Sixteen, seventeen…to the back wall of the entry hall. Hmm … a long runner? Maybe just a large rug in the center of the entrance with a round table. We could install textured wall covering here at the back. As I measure the back wall, I notice a thin line running between panels of wainscoting under the stairs. A hollow sound reverberates as I tap near the seam. No knob, no hinges … . With a hunch, I quickly push on the edge of the panel, and voilà, the wall pops ajar. Squeaking the wall open, a small toilet room is revealed. Shaking my head, I write **case of WD-40.**

Reverently turning the key in the lock, Josh and I step back from the doors and look up. This is the house we had always dreamed of but never been able to find. After Josh and I bonded over French food and wine, we enjoyed many a holiday jaunt in France. The French cuisine and culture beckoned, and we yearned to make the country our home. Paris was exciting, filled with restaurants, stores, architecture, and history! But alas, the winters are cold and gloomy. Lyon, of course, met our gastronomic requirements and brought back memories of my studies, but it didn't feel right for our life together. Over the years, we read real estate listings and dreamed, but could never seem to find a place that called to us, until Wendy's video tour of the villa.

This villa isn't in a city. There is no cultural center to speak of, and yet, something speaks to us both. Our souls have found home. This is to be our home and new adventure, and we are thrilled about it.

Stomachs filled with cassoulet; we snuggled under a warm down comforter. That was hours ago. Tossing and turning next to a soundly sleeping partner is annoying. Josh breathes rhythmically, occasionally mumbling. So far, I've been able to make out the words stove, sink, and roast chicken. I don't need to hear them, though, to know he's dreaming about his new kitchen. I can hear the tone of his voice. Even in his sleep, the energy that lights him up when he "talks food," especially French food, is carrying him away. He goes to a place in his soul where nothing else exists. That energy fills him, and when he shares it, I am carried away too. In addition to being well fed, life with Josh has filled me with joy.

I smile for him and pat him as thoughts of the day overwhelm me. Today, I felt as though I had been floating through a dream. And at the same time being attacked by thoughts of "how can we do this?" How do we get a bathroom in all six rooms on the first floor? How do we make space for the four of us AND guests? We will surely need more electric service. Where do we even begin with that? Do we need to add another sewage system? Was that a grey water line I saw running out of the prep kitchen into the garden?

What will we find when we begin rearranging walls? There had been no reports of plumbing or electrical problems during the inspection, but let's be real. The last time the villa was updated, there were three toilets, two bathing areas, and a kitchen sink without a disposal. The ancient knob and tube wiring efficiently handled the limited number of electrical plugs. It's just too much to think about tonight. Tomorrow, we will see the French architect; he will surely have answers.

As I try to sleep, horror stories of hard-to-find artisans who leave unfinished work in their wake haunt me. I know Josh meant well when he bought me Peter Mayle's *A Year in Provence* for the plane ride over, but right now the fear of repeating the author's travails is driving me crazy. I do need to sleep.

Finally, I am floating off to sleep thinking about remodeling the servants' quarters into private quarters for the four of us, and it hits me. I have retired to become a vassal to this grand *maison*. I let the thought sink in, and something in my body says, "This feels right." Thinking of the thick walls and firm foundation of the villa gives me a feeling of grounding that tells me it's OK to dream of a future here.

4

Vibrations of the Land

Pomme, April 2011

Sunlight glinting off a passing car catches my eye.

"Look, André, another tourist come to spend their American dollars in your café! No, wait. There they go. Our little town is too small for them to stop. Maybe next time you'll get lucky."

Setting my coffee on the table, André looks up just as the car turns the corner. "Pomme, I think those are the Americans who have bought the villa."

My belly tightens. New owners of the villa? Americans? Non!

It's been 4 years since Madame passed, and we've all kept watch on Bonne Vie. The summer before last, when the drought took hold and it seemed that even the old fig might not survive, I found hoses in the garden shed and flooded the grounds, one metre at a time. I refused to allow Madame's Garden to die. Each day, I watered; Le Chat watched me from the roof like a judge deciding if I was worthy of the task. My Chien's barking from the ground didn't help my case, I'm sure.

Last fall, there had been rumours of new owners. But who can believe rumours? Even so, I should have heard more about this. Twice a week, André and I keep our appointment for coffee. First, I see Colette at the boulangerie for my fresh baguette. As is her habit, she tosses in an old loaf for the birds and happily dispenses a treat to Chien. Ambling over the cobblestones, Chien and I settle at André's for espresso and news of the world. Over the years, André and I have watched the tourists during the summer and in the winter shared stories from our past. But I had not heard this news of the villa. How had I missed that?

Walking home, I glance up the drive of the villa. Years of unpruned willow trees sway in the wind as the tips of their branches sweep the drive, and this spring's crop of weeds freshly watered by spring rains creates an impenetrable veil shrouding everything beyond the dip in the drive. Who are these new owners? What are their plans for the villa?

My heart aches as I think of how the world has changed. Both Madame and Monsieur are gone, as I fear is the magic of this place. Their passing released me from my promise, but does it release me from my debt? I shake my head, knowing that only when I return to the ground will I be free.

As a child, life was not easy. With little space and even less money, Maman had no time to attend to the restlessness of her fourth son. Wandering the streets was easier than fighting for what little there was at home, my hunger a constant gnawing within me. And then my life changed.

That evening, the twilight and crisp air told me it was time to head home. Without thought, I allowed my feet to carry me in that direction. Head down, my eyes following the stone. Noticing a change in their pattern. I looked up to find myself outside of Monsieur Bloch's estate. To a six-year-old, the garden walls were massive. The branches of apple trees filled with sweet ripe fruit were all I could see above me. A force drew me to the wall as the gnawing within me whispered, "You can do it. The wall's not that high. One apple, just one. No one will notice."

On the other side of the wall, Monsieur Bloch was planning his harvest, and I, in my hunger, didn't notice him. I reached out my hand, my mouth watering at the thought of the apple. Just as I pulled the fruit from its branch, his firm hand clasped my wrist. Mute with fear, I froze. Pulling my scrawny body down from the top of the wall, he looked me over, dirty, dressed in little more than rags, knobby knees and elbows peeking out of holes. Monsieur Bloch released my wrist. "Unless you want to visit the gendarmerie, I expect to see you at my door tomorrow after school. Do you understand?" I nodded. Shaking, but with apple in hand, I quickly scuttled back over the wall and down the street.

The next day, and almost every day after, I appeared at M. Bloch's door. Each time I arrived, there was a job to be done. One day, I would pick apples; another day, I would spread straw over the plants to prepare them for the winter. While the Mistral blew across the land, I cleaned and repaired equipment, sorted seeds, and eventually planted them in the greenhouse, where I learned to wait patiently for new life. On Saturdays, M. Bloch insisted that we rest and reflect. As we walked around the estate M. Bloch shared stories about the garden, the fruit trees he had planted as a young man, the tomatoes that he had begun in his garden shed when the snow still covered the ground, or the flowers he had planted outside the kitchen window when he brought his new wife home.

Working with M. Bloch had its own soundtrack —a low, vibrating hum that emanated from his stocky body as he worked. The soothing vibrations seemed to push their way up from the ground, rumble around inside his barrel chest, and then float from his throat. It was as though he was plugged into the land that he tended. His hymn of contentment filled the air, whether we were turning soil, pulling weeds, or carefully pruning grape vines on the trellis.

When I left each day, I was granted an apple, a cabbage, a few potatoes, something to keep my hunger at bay. In the beginning, I worked to avoid the gendarmerie; as time passed, I worked to avoid hunger. But in the end, it was M. Bloch's kindness and attention that drew me back to the garden.

As I grew older, I was entrusted with increasingly larger responsibilities. The year I turned nine M. Bloch told me that I was free to gather the apples that had fallen from the trees and take them home. The first few baskets filled Maman's pies and sauces. Then I began selling them to neighbours and eventually sold them at the farmers' market. I didn't just sell the apples. I promoted them. I was the Johnny Appleseed of France, sharing information about the type of apple I was selling, when that tree had come into bloom, how long it had taken to ripen, how to store the apples, and sometimes I'd even share one of Maman's recipes. By the time I was ten, everyone called me Pomme.

During my tenth year, things in our town began to change. Even the strong garden walls couldn't protect us from the storm that had been brewing all over Europe. There were days I worked alone in the garden, the house dark. When M. Bloch joined me, he was quiet and preoccupied. I missed his humming. The last day we were in the garden together, I caught the glint of tears in his eyes. I wish I had had the words to reach out, but what does a ten-year-old boy know about the tears of old men?

I didn't understand why Monsieur Bloch left our town, his garden, and me. I knew of the rumblings to the east, but my ten-year-old mind could not comprehend the effect they had on M. Bloch or his family. There finally came the day that the gates were locked, the house lifeless. I could have climbed the wall as I had so many years ago, but this time I couldn't bring myself to do it.

Without the connection to the land, the gnawing inside me returned. Walking the woods and country paths was not enough. I needed to plug into the earth. I needed to feel the vibration of life, the soil in my hands. That fall a few neighbors allowed me to help with their harvests and prepare their beds for the coming cold, but the need to nurture my own garden tore at my insides like a beast struggling to be free.

I found myself once again wandering the countryside. Maybe it was the wall that slowed my step; the memory of another wall awakened within me. Where the stone turned away from the road, I stopped to survey the land. Just beyond the estate lay a field that had been left to its own devices—a few brambles grew wildly near the creek just before the woods. Early thistles stretched towards the spring sun as butterflies fluttered between patches of garrigue and lavender. Inhaling the spring air, I absent-mindedly reached down to pull a weed from a lavender patch. Wandering on, I cut a few stems of rosemary and thyme to take to Maman. The gnawing feeling was lost to thoughts of the land.

The next day, I cleared a path to the brambles and pulled away the weeds. Another day, I found a young olive tree hidden among the scrub. Each time I returned, the gnawing lessened, and the humming grew.

The patch of land began to take shape. In a clear area not too far from the creek, I tended a few squash, tomato, and aubergine seedlings I had pulled from a neighbour's garden when I helped him thin his newly sprouted rows. I nurtured the vegetables, carrying water from the creek, pulling weeds, and humming the song of life into their stems.

Monsieur, whose wall I passed each day, must surely own the land, but he never interfered with my garden. One day I arrived to find an old spade lying at the edge of the squash vines. A few days later, a rake leaned against the support pole of an aubergine and when the sun grew to bake the land, a bucket, much larger than the broken pot I had been using, appeared. With each appearance, my job became easier, and my garden more vibrant. At the end of the first summer, I left a basket of squash, tomatoes, and aubergine at the kitchen door of the villa as a thank you and the only payment I could offer.

During the war years, the garden kept our family alive, but I was always sure to deliver regular baskets to the villa's kitchen door. After six years of tending to this patch of land outside the wall, my garden had become very productive, not only feeding me but also supporting my mother and younger brother. When I was eighteen, Monsieur sent word that he wanted to see me. In all those years, I had never seen him, much less spoken to him.

Filled with guilt and fear, I entered the gates of Bonne Vie. In the grand foyer, I was overcome with awe, my feet barely able to follow the butler into Monsieur's office. A tall, thin gentleman inclined to few words, Monsieur was a mystery. There were whispers around town that he was of royal blood, a descendant of the house of Chalon-Arlay. He could even lay claim to the title Prince of Orange, but he had fallen in love with Madame and made a life here far from the drama of royalty.

Monsieur rose as I entered. He greeted me with a nod of the head and a firm handshake. "Pomme, I have taken notice of the garden you have grown outside my wall."

Oh no, here it comes…

"I am impressed with the love you have for the land and the care that you give it. You have shown yourself to be persistent and industrious. And from what my cook tells me, a supplier of quality vegetables."

"Oui, monsieur," I stammered.

"How would you like to own that land?"

"Monsieur? Oh, sir, I have no money to pay you. With my father and older brothers gone, I am the only support of my mother and younger brother."

"I am aware of your situation, but I feel someone who works as hard as you do deserves to work his own land."

"Monsieur? What could he mean?"

Handing me a piece of paper, he said, "This should adequately cover the situation."

I held the paper before me, the letters swirled before my eyes as my heart raced, and my tongue stuck to the roof of my mouth.

"There are a lot of legal words there. What they say is that the plot of land on which your garden sits is to be yours. You are to pay for it through regular deliveries of fruits and vegetables to my kitchen, a small monthly payment from the money you make selling your produce, and odd jobs that my gardener requests of you here at the villa."

In that moment, I became a landowner. I had a place in the community. My gratitude to Monsieur was boundless. Though we never spoke again, whenever we passed in town, he would nod his head in acknowledgement.

As a landowner, I could plan for a future on MY land. I began gathering timber, discarded bricks, stone, and other building supplies. A small hut in which I stored my tools turned into a slightly larger cottage. Over the years, both my home and my garden grew, as did my business at the weekly market. It was at the market that I lost myself in Lizette's deep brown eyes.

A tingle travels up my arm, and the knot in my throat catches whatever words I might have thought to say. Our hands brush as I hand her the radishes I've set aside for her. Last week, those beautiful brown eyes had been filled with disappointment when she realized she'd arrived too late. My delicately flavored spring radishes are coveted and not many make it to market after the villa receives its share and André's father gets his box for the café. But radishes aren't the only things I've set aside for the girl with the beautiful brown eyes and shy smile. Back during truffle season, I slipped one of the earthy nobs into her bag of potatoes and last spring I saved the best pears for her. I watch her make her way through the crowd, my emotions swirling and while I wished I knew the words to match them.

André laughs when I tell him of my struggle, but unlike Cyrano, he has no helpful words.

"Ask her to coffee at the end of market day."

"And what would I say, nice coffee?"

"You can tell her about your garden. God knows I've listened to enough about it over the years."

"She doesn't want to hear about planting potatoes and spreading compost."

"Talk about the radishes. Tell her about apples, Pomme."

"My lips struggle to form words when she's around."

"Then just let her talk. She is a girl."

On a rainy spring day when everyone shops quickly and stands close early, I ask Lizette to have coffee at the café. We shyly eye one another, and it is André who opens the door.

"Pomme, Maman made this tart from the strawberries you brought her this morning. She wants to know what you put in the soil this year. She says they're your best crop ever." He sets a slice of tart before us.

Placing a piece of tart in her mouth, Lizette closes her eyes as she savours the fruit. Suddenly her eyes pop open and she is looking directly into mine.

"These strawberries are wonderful! What is your secret?"

After that there is no stopping me. The secrets of my garden flow from my heart to hers. From that day on, we met at the café after the market to share a coffee and André's mother's latest treat, lost in the dreams my words were painting.

When I turned twenty, we married, and my house became a home.

Time passed. I added rooms, Lizette filled them with love, and together we raised two children on this land.

Through the years, I delivered a weekly basket to the kitchen door of the villa. During the summer, the basket overflowed with bounty from my garden. During the leaner months, I foraged for berries, snails, ramps, or truffles. Sometimes Lizette baked a cake, but every week there was a basket, and with the food, an envelope holding a payment for my land.

In his 85th year, Monsieur passed away. The sadness at the villa enveloped the village. Three months later, the mayor arrived at my door with an envelope. In the envelope was the deed to my land, along with a note written by Monsieur. "Thank you for being a faithful neighbor, and a caring custodian of the land." Monsieur had seen to it that I received the deed to this land, though I knew I had not fully paid my debt. I knew I never would be able to repay all that Monsieur's faith in me was worth. Until the day Madame drew her final breath, there was a weekly basket at the kitchen door of the villa.

In the years that followed Monsieur's death, life in the village fell into a new rhythm. The spirit of Monsieur was carried in our hearts, all of us were determined to see that Madame was cared for, and that the villa was maintained.

A decade after Monsieur died, an illness we never understood struck my sweet Lizette. One day she was humming as she baked pies and cakes for the holidays, and the next she was unable to leave her bed. In the spring, she was gone, leaving holes in our hearts and in disbelief that her warmth and joy would no longer fill our lives. The melody of the land left me and tending the soil became a labor with no love. During those dark days, my children tried to convince me to move to Nantes or Toulouse to live near one of them.

"You can sell the land, Papa, and get an apartment near one of us. You won't have to work, and we could see you more often."

Even if Lizette had taken my heart and its melody with her, I knew I could never leave the land. I would not abandon Madame or my promise to Monsieur. I would stay.

When Madame died the following year, I thought my heart would break, and I was sure it was time for my body to return to the earth. I could barely drag myself from bed, and bending to tend the garden, found me stuck somewhere between upright and the soil. Many days, I just wandered the rows, kicking at the weeds. Until the day Chien entered the garden.

The day is warm and sunny. The world is returning to life, the garden turning a bright green in the spring. I slowly hoe the newly sprouted radishes, lost in a memory of Lizette's eyes. Barking shakes me from my reverie. There is a dog running about my garden chasing an Azur de Trèfle that flits from flower to flower, zigging and zagging, flying up and down just avoiding the dog's yapping mouth. I laugh, and the sound startles me. I can't remember the last time my body made that sound. The dog jumps and whirls in mid-air as if imitating the path of the butterfly. His landing is not as graceful, and a full-bellied guffaw escapes my body. Shaking the dust from himself the dog trots over, plops down before me and cocks his head.

"Ah, Chien, thank you for reminding me how to laugh."

Turning back to my hoe, I address the weeds with more vigour than I have known in a year, the old melody seeping up from the earth into my body. Chien watches as I turn up weedy sprouts, moving down the row with me, I the worker and he the appreciative observer.

"OK, boy, we've come to the end of the row; you can scamper on home now."

Chien looks up the next row and back to me as if to say, "We're not done yet."

Shrugging, I begin the new row, and our two-car train chugs on under the warm spring sun. And thus, we complete my chores for the day.

Chien meets me at the door the next morning and follows me to where the asparagus has sprouted another day's meal. When I lean down to cut the bright green stems, Chien happily licks my face as if to say good morning before trotting to a tree to relieve himself.

"Lizette, it looks as though this funny ball of fur has claimed a new home." A warmth fills me, and I know my new companion's arrival is no accident.

The vibration of the land has returned to my life.

5

Love's Return

FABIAN—LE JARDINIER, MAY 2011

BUSHY THYME PLANTS HUM WITH BEES AS I PASS, AND THE SCENT of lavender wafts through the air. In my mind, I am a child tagging along after my father. It is that wonderful time of year when the buds of spring are about to burst into the lushness of summer. Color is everywhere, and from my five-year-old point of view, I am swimming in a sea of brilliant greens, yellows, pinks, and purples. Lost in this maze of color, I skip happily behind the butterflies as they flutter from blossom to blossom. The light, the color, the scents will become the very essences of my life. It is that day that the plants, the insects, and the sun wound their way into my soul, and my future was set. I would follow my father's footsteps and become le jardinier.

My father's journey at the villa began the spring after the Nazi tide receded. On that day, Papa was returning from Deschamps's farm, where he had hoped to find work helping with spring planting. But he was not alone in his quest. By the time he made it to the front of the line, the jobs for that day had been filled.

"But I must work!"

"Maybe tomorrow, mon ami."

With a heavy heart, Papa turned away. Mimi's queasy stomach won't be satisfied with day-old bread much longer. As soon as this sickness passes, she will need food for herself and the child she carries. They are my responsibility. I will return tomorrow, much earlier.

Returning home, Papa passed the villa where a movement caught his eye and pulled him from his thoughts. Someone was struggling to pull a dead limb from a tree just inside the wall. Papa stepped onto the grounds, took hold, and with one swift pull brought down the floundering branch

"Thank you for your assistance," the man nodded as he straightened his waistcoat.

Papa was taken aback; it was Monsieur himself.

"Avec plaisir, Monsieur." Papa nodded and turned to leave. Scanning the grounds, he saw more heavy branches dangling from trees like specters of paratroopers whose shoots have carried them awry. "Would you like some help with those?" he asked, nodding towards the nearest dangling limb.

Monsieur surveyed the garden. "What do you think about taking care of the rest of the spring clean-up?"

"Oui, Monsieur." The two walked to the garden shed.

"I believe you will find the tools you need in here. Let me know when you're done, and we'll figure out what I owe you."

"Merci." The two men shook hands, and Monsieur returned to the house.

After stacking the dead branches near the gate, Papa returned to the shack. Rake in hand, he exited the hut and nearly collided with the cook who was standing in the door.

"Monsieur asked me to bring you un peu de nourriture." Glancing around, she continued, "It looks like you have plenty of work ahead of you. You will need this." Handing him a cup of coffee and a small baguette filled with a fried egg, she returned to the kitchen.

Mimi should be the one eating this, thought Papa. Leaving the empty cup on the step to the kitchen door, he returned to his work. Carefully, he raked the leaves that shrouded spring buds unfolding from the ground. Lost in thought, Papa didn't hear the leaves crackle until a woman was standing next to him. He looked up to find a petite woman, burlap sack in hand. She smiled. "I do hope you can help me with these. I know a bit about flowers and herbs, but I'm afraid I'm not too good with grape vines."

"Oui, Madame, I'll see what I can do."

Tenderly handing him the bag, she smiled again and walked toward the house. Grape vines, what do I do with them? he thought. Finding a bucket in the shed, Papa filled it with water and left the vines to soak. Returning to his work, he contemplated his situation. We all know how to pick grapes, but I have no idea how to plant them. Maybe I can get Mario to help me.

Before the war, Mario worked at Maison Roche. He will know what to do, but will he want to talk about being a vigneron? He was the foreman there. No one will forget that. The whole town took notice when old man Roche hired Mario just after high school. Before that, Maison Roche was like every other vineyard; the family did the work, except at harvest time when we all pitched in. Taking on a full-time employee might have seemed pretentious had it not been for the way the old man and Mario got along, walking the fields shoulder to shoulder, the sage imparting his knowledge to the pupil. They were so close that no one would have been surprised had Richard Roche adopted Mario.

As the old man aged, more of the care of the fields fell to Mario. When the old man died in '38 and Emile, the oldest son, took over, it looked as though Mario was destined to remain part of the family. On his deathbed, Richard made Emile promise that Maison Roche would remain a family business and that all the family members would play a part in it. True to his word, Emile consulted his brother Lucas on business decisions and depended on Mario for advice on the fields.

The family worked together, and Maison Roche continued to grow. All was well until the Germans invaded Poland in '39, and Mario, a staunch defender of la République, joined the army to protect his country. Like all times of nationalistic fervor, fighting for one's country was all that was discussed; memories of a war in the not-too-distant past faded into the background. France was turning out to defend an ally, so, of course, God was on her side.

The story we all told had Mario back tending the vines before the next harvest. And at first, that's what it looked like. The battlefront grew quiet, and people began to call it the war that wasn't a war. Until the blitzkrieg. Overnight, it seemed, France was no longer at war with Germany, and the Vichy government was running the country, at least the part of it that the Nazis weren't interested in.

Whether Mario saw it as luck or not, he had been injured by a grenade explosion and taken from the front before the Germans began rounding up French soldiers as prisoners of war. Declared a wounded veteran, Mario returned to our small town of L'Esprit du Rhône and his work in the fields, but he was never the same.

A piece of shrapnel lodged in his right hip left him with a limp, but the real wound went deeper, the wound to Mario's heart over what his country had become. Mario carried his disappointment on his sleeve and often clashed with Lucas, who insisted that Mario had lost interest in working. Emile stood between the two as much as he could. He valued Mario's knowledge and respected him for the time he had spent at the front. Besides, Mario was part of the family, and Emile knew his father would want him to be there. As the Vichy government grew more aligned with the Nazis, Mario grew more unhappy.

Depending on who you asked, Mario quit, or Lucas fired him. Either way, Mario and Maison Roche parted ways.

Not long afterwards, Mario disappeared. Not even his family knew where he had gone. Because he had spoken often of his vision of France, the country of Liberté, Égalité & Fraternité, people wondered if he hadn't gone off to join de Gaulle, but no one knew for sure. When the Vichy and later the Nazis inquired about his whereabouts, the truth was that no one knew.

Mario's mother died late in '41, and everyone was sure he would make his way back to L'Esprit du Rhône. Even the Nazis thought so. Just before the funeral, a small contingent of soldiers arrived in town. They hung around for a month before giving up. Talk around town was divided.

"Mario must surely be dead. What son misses his mother's funeral? "

"How could he even know she is dead? He is in England with de Gaulle!"

One thing both camps agreed on was that Mario would never return to L'Esprit du Rhône.

But return he did. One cold, clear day in December, after the Allied invasion and de Gaulle's establishment of the Provisional Government, Mario appeared. The town's people were stunned, but his family joyously embraced the son who had seemingly risen from the dead. For the first few weeks, there were many questions about where he had been and what he had done, but no matter who asked, the answer was the same: silence.

"It's just the trauma of the war," people said. "Once he heals, he will tell us."

But it had been over six months, and still Mario had nothing to say about where he was, who he was with, or what he did, so we no longer ask.

Papa hesitantly approached Mario with his request for help with planting the vines. The words hung between them, and the silence froze them each in his place. Papa was about to turn away when a sad smile came to Mario's face.

"Yes, I can help you."

Though he didn't speak of the old man directly, Mario's face reflected fond memories of his time at the old man's side. Slowly, Mario outlined the steps Papa should take to prepare the soil and vines for planting. At times, his eyes glistened with tears. There were occasional pauses while L'Esprit du Rhône's most stoic veteran became lost in thought, looking away as though reliving days he and Richard Roche had walked the fields together, the love of his master warming his heart.

When Mario finished, Papa quietly thanked him and turned to leave.

"It is I who should thank you for rekindling a love I had forgotten."

Unable to find the words to respond, Papa swallowed hard and nodded. Papa was sure that Mario never lost his love for Maison Roche. The real reason for his departure lay somewhere deep within his broken heart.

The next day, stepping back to admire his work and saying a prayer that the vines survive, Papa heard a voice over his shoulder.

"Those vines are much like the people of France. We have survived the worst, and although our land is scarred, we will grow strong again."

Papa turned to see Monsieur silently taking in the ragged vines that barely extend above the soil.

Monsieur continued, "The land will heal more quickly than our hearts and souls. It's the beauty of the land that will bring us the hope we need." Looking up from the vines, he continued. "Let's begin that hope right here. Since Louis left, the garden has been adrift. How would you like to stay on and watch those vines grow? And nurture the hope our country needs so badly?"

That was the day my father became le jardinier at Bonne Vie and the day that Bonne Vie began to nurture me.

That spring, Madame decided the beauty should begin in the form of a newly planted herb and flower garden and a few vegetables. Paths of crushed rock guided visitors through bushy thyme, poms poms of alum, tall shoots of dill, tendrils of pea plants, roses on their trellises, and tall sunflowers reaching towards the sky.

At the end of that first summer, they planned the fruit orchard. Madame was especially fond of apricots, so there had to be two trees, one to enjoy during the season and the other to preserve so she could enjoy their bright sweetness when the Mistral blew through the land and summer was but a distant memory. The list continued with trees of almond, apple, pear, plum, peach, and fig. The fig tree would of course be given its own space—near the corner of the wall to protect it from the winter winds, but not too close to the rest of the garden so that the tree would have space to unfurl its ranging branches and broad leaves. And of course, there were the blackberry brambles that grew up the trellis on the sunny side of the garden shed, the strawberry plants in the raised garden, and the grape vines that covered the wall.

The olive trees were the old timers on the estate. They had been there when the villa was built. Folklore has it that they were remnants of an old Roman olive grove that had been protected and passed down from generation to generation, with the understanding that no olive tree was to be cut down until its leaves grew no more. Over the years, a few of them had lost their place for a road or a wall, but you are just as likely to run upon a road that takes a curve for no apparent reason before returning to its logical path. The olive tree around which the road had been built has long since lost its leaves, but today, the flow of traffic continues to pay it tribute.

As the garden grew, so did I. Years passed, and my visits to the garden became more frequent. My early springs were spent following my father's hoe, dropping seeds in the newly furrowed soil, and gently patting dirt back into place. All summer I chased butterflies and collected beetles. In the fall my pockets would bulge with walnuts. Madame would laugh and call me her little squirrel with pockets. One summer, Madame gave me an old jar in which to store my specimens. I carried that jar with me everywhere that summer, never knowing what interesting insect I might find. One morning, as I sat on the steps to the kitchen door, Pomme appeared with his basket of vegetables for the cook.

"That's quite a collection you have there." He bent nearer, tousled my hair, and whispered, "Now don't you go getting yourself lost. I've already returned one little boy to the villa." Chuckling to himself, he strolled off. What a queer thing to say. I knew the woods around Bonne Vie almost as well as this garden. Shrugging, I returned to my collection.

When I finished school, there was no question of my vocation. I apprenticed myself to my father, and Monsieur kindly allotted a few francs more to his garden budget. When I turned nineteen, I reluctantly left the comfort of Monsieur's walls to work around the Vaucluse. During those years, I helped with harvests, planted small gardens for homeowners, installed trees ordered from the pépinière, and even worked as a vigneron for a short time. Though this experience taught me much, my heart remained tied to the garden of my youth.

My return to the garden came unexpectedly. On a sunny spring afternoon, 25 years after stepping into the walls of the estate, my father's spirit left this world for the next. While walking the grounds, planning his work for another year, his heart stopped. His passing left a hole in my heart, our family without a provider, and Monsieur sans jardinier. It was with mixed emotions that I stepped into my destiny as le jardinier at the villa. In the garden, I found the strength and the peace to go on. With every step I took, I felt my father. The breeze fluttering through the leaves called his name. The scent of the lavender lining the paths set my heart at peace, and the sun reminded me of the warmth of his hugs as if to say, "I am here. All is well."

The first two years after Madame's passing, the bank paid me to care for the house and garden on a weekly basis. The board at the bank was sure its beauty would quickly enchant a new owner. As the years went on and the economy seemed to move in reverse, the executors of Madame's will grew less enchanted with making a good deal and more concerned with pennies saved. Although their checks stopped coming, I didn't. I no longer had as much time to tend to the garden and keep up with house repairs, but I did stop by regularly to see that the water from the rain barrel seeped into the cat's bowl and to visit with Madame's lonely guardian. Le Chat and I shared lunch in the shade of the orchard, me dropping bits of saucisson and fromage for her, and she rubbing against my leg in appreciation. We enjoyed the butterflies and bees during the summers, the colorful leaves in the fall, and huddled in a sunny spot in the lee of the house when the Mistral blew. Just as I could never completely abandon this place, Le Chat would never patrol another garden.

Happily, Le Chat and the garden have found a new mistress. The new mistress is enchanted with her Eden and wants to know it better before considering any changes. This season, I am tasked with removing debris, pulling weeds, and restoring the crispness to the lines of the path. As for the herbs that didn't survive the years of abandonment, the new mistress will plant them - under the watchful eye of Le Chat, I am sure. I will send Gerard to restore Madame's fountain to its lively self. He, too, will be happy to see the sparkle return to the garden.

My heart sighs in relief, having met the villa's new residents. I say residents, because no one can truly own this place. This stately, yet warm and inviting home draws its energy from the land and in return provides the land a reason for being. When Madame passed away four years ago, the town mourned her loss and worried about what that loss would mean for the magic that emanated from these walls. As time went on, the villa continued to live, not only in the memories of the old, but as a placeholder in time and a symbol of all that could be right in the world.

Now that I've met the unlikely foursome who occupy the villa, I believe they are who the house has been waiting for. These Americans have much to learn about living in France, and the stories steeped in the walls of the villa. But the joy these foreigners bring with them has already filled the rooms of the house. It flows out into the garden, reminding us all why the dip in the drive remains.

Love has returned.

6

Maison Roche

CAMILLE, JUNE 2011

Stupid Americans! They have no idea what they're doing, even the one who likes to think he's French. All he could do was nod and say oui, oui. Camille could hear his silly voice in her head as she stomped through the fields. "I'll have to talk to my friends before I can decide something like that."

Such a simple decision, and he can't make it! I thought Americans were smarter. Maybe it's just living in that house. This bunch is comme des imbéciles as the old man and old lady were. Everyone thought that the archaic couple was so special. When Madame finally passed away, people were sure the village would fall apart. Well, she's been gone five years now, and we're doing just fine, thank you. No! We're doing better. No more bowing and scraping to those royal wannabes. Who did they think they were, sitting in that big house of theirs looking down on the rest of us?

Kicking at clods of earth, Camille storms through the field, a cloud of dust engulfing her, marking her passage between the vines.

Even Uncle Emile bowed to them. It should have been him she married. That Monsieur was a nobody. Uncle Emile, the most eligible bachelor around, should have been the one she married instead of some tall, dour stranger who promised her a mansion. She could have shared Uncle Emile's dreams for the vineyard and helped him build what grand père had begun. But no, she decided to be the bride of a man who passed himself off as nobility. The bastard of a noble, maybe, but not a man of title. Besides, this is France. We took care of that kind two hundred years ago.

Camille wipes the sweat from her eyes as she climbs the hill towards the winery.

If only Fabien hadn't come to feed le Chat that day, this problem would have been over. The house was abandoned, and no one was even looking at it anymore. All I had to do was pull out the vines and be on my way, problem solved. But no, that sentimental gardener arrived before I could remove even one of those stolen vines. Those vines belong to Maison Roche. If Uncle Emile hadn't been under that woman's spell, he wouldn't have given them to her all those years ago. What did he see in her? She didn't deserve his love and undying loyalty. He knew he couldn't win her heart with those roots; she'd been married to The Monsieur for years by then. She had no interest in him or our family. The country was rebuilding after the war, and the Roche family was on its way to becoming the giant it is today. He should have turned his back on her.

Stopping to catch her breath, Camille looks over Maison Roche's fields. The calming energy of the land begins to creep into her body, but she isn't ready to release her anger and stomps on.

The Madam wouldn't have wandered by while Uncle Emile was planting had he not chosen that field on the edge of the property. Papa thought Uncle Emile was crazy to be planting our best root stock there. It was poor land even by Provençal standards, and Papa was sure the vines wouldn't see enough sunlight for the grapes to sweeten. When Papa discovered his older brother had spent an entire week in that field, he was furious. "What a waste of time! You are dreaming if you think anything will come of that scrap of land."

According to the family story, Uncle Emile replied, "Then it will be my field of lost dreams."

What Papa didn't know was that Uncle Emile's field of lost dreams would end up producing the best wine in the Maison Roche collection.

Uncle Emile always did have a sense of what was good when it came to grapes, though Papa could never admit it.

Exhausted from her march, Camille sits on a rock in the shade of an overhanging cliff. She hadn't planned on visiting the villa today. She'd been out walking the fields; her head filled with numbers. She begins to contemplate:

How much money would the newest agreement with the American wine dealer bring in?

How many bottles would this year's harvest yield?

Will there be enough bottles to meet the deal?

How highly will the newly bottled wine be rated?

Will they remain the highest-rated in the Côtes du Rhône?

But most importantly, how much can we charge for the newest Rêves Perdu? We need the increased income to cover the expense of the updated facilities. To demand that price, Rêves Perdu must remain exclusive and limited.

Exclusive and limited, that's the key to our success. Except those vines at the villa are from the same root stock as our Rêves Perdu, and their placement against that wall at the side of the house means they receive the same limited sunlight as our grapes. Those vines produce fruit like ours. The difference is that we know how to turn our grapes into wine, and they don't. But if those Americans were to find themselves a vintner, there could be competition. Having to compete with our OWN grapes would be ridiculous! Had Uncle Emile demanded the return of the vines as Papa told him to, there would be no problem.

Oh, how I remember that day. The day that Uncle Emile returned from Bonne Vie empty-handed. I had been playing in the garden and ran happily to greet my favorite person in the world, my Uncle Emile. Before he could pick me up, I could feel a change in the air. Papa was demanding something of Uncle Emile. In fear, I ran to my mother. From behind her skirts, I watched as Papa's face grew red with rage.

"Again? You have chosen that woman over the family again?"

I shook with fear as the argument between the two men I loved grew worse. I was afraid that Papa would lash out, and Uncle Emile would respond. Although Uncle Emile, the larger of the two, had always been the peacemaker, I could see he was losing his patience at having the same argument, yet again. His feelings for the Madam were none of his brother's business and had nothing to do with the agreement he had made with Monsieur. Monsieur had agreed not to sell their wine, and that was good enough. Uncle Emile knew Monsieur to be a man of his word. Maison Roche would not have to worry about competition from the Bonne Vie Villa.

Uncle Emile had said all there was to say about the vines at Bonne Vie and turned his back on the argument. Since Grand-père's death, Uncle Emile had gone out of his way to include Papa in decisions concerning the winery, though everyone knew who legally had the last word. There was nothing Papa could do about Uncle Emile's agreement with Monsieur. It took weeks before Papa and Uncle Emile spoke again, and eventually life went back to normal, though the strain between the two never completely healed. Papa refused to trust Monsieur or Madame, and that distrust lasted until Papa's last breath.

When Uncle Emile died, the year after Monsieur, Papa decided he would go to the villa to demand that the old lady stop making wine. With both Monsieur and Emile out of the way, he was sure he would be able to accomplish what Uncle Emile should have years before. Papa even supplied the old bat with an excuse. With Monsieur gone, surely Madame wouldn't be entertaining anymore. She didn't need so many bottles of wine every year, especially since she was giving most of them away. Did she listen to reason? NO! She smiled at Papa and told him that she was sure both Monsieur and Uncle Emile would want her to continue to share her bounty.

She and her free wine made us the laughingstock of the Côtes du Rhône. People would brag about having received a bottle of the best wine in the region as a gift from Madame. Recipients of the gift invariably held tastings to compare Bonne Vie's wine with ours. The tastings always ended in favor of Bonne Vie. Of Course, they chose

Bonne Vie, the wine had been free! That nonsense didn't end until the old lady died. That's when people began hoarding their bottles. And the bottles in the villa's cellar? That banker De la Cour swooped in and carted them away. No one knows how many bottles are still out there. No one will sell them, though. They couldn't bear to part with a gift from Madame. Good, they can keep their bottles hidden, and we will sell our Rêves Perdus at the price it deserves."

Camille shakes her head, and her thoughts shift to the present.

However, with the expanded sales agreement in America, we could use the grapes produced at the villa. We could call the wine Rêves Perdus II. The very limited production would make the bottles even more valuable. Americans like to believe they have something rare and special. It's incredible how much they are willing to pay for a bottle they don't think anyone else will have.

The expansion of business in America is making it harder to meet shipping requests from Germany. Had I not promised Papa to continue doing business with his friends in Germany, I would have dropped them as soon as the American markets took off. I don't know who Papa's friend was, but his children are not easy to work with. They act as if I owe them something, always bargaining for lower prices and taking a larger share of the profits. At least their new agent is easier to work with. He doesn't act as though speaking French is below him. Maybe it was the attitude of Papa's friends that made Uncle Emile refuse to let Papa do business in Germany. I never did understand the problem, but their conversations about any business in Germany were cold and stilted and always ended with Uncle Emile announcing, "That connection ended in Paris in 1951."

Camille steps into the shade of the oldest building in the vineyard. Breathing deeply, her shoulders relax, and the cool of the shade refreshes her. Her thoughts begin to wander again.

This is where it all began. Richard Roche, my grand-père, built this structure to protect his first tractor. Later, he built walls around all four sides and moved wine production from the kitchen to its own space. Grand père's skills as a vintner are renowned. When he was young, he was known all over the Vaucluse and half of the Gard region. Expanding Maison Roche's grape production and redirecting the family business from fruits and vegetables to solely grapes and wine production made sense.

How I wish I had known him. The stories I have heard about my grand-père are of a jovial man who loved people. People say to know Uncle Emile was to know Richard Roche. Everyone loved them both. I suppose I'm lucky to be named after Uncle Emile. When Maman delivered me, she was told not to bear another child if she valued her life, so my naming became a significant topic of conversation. It was obvious that Uncle Emile would never marry and have children of his own. With me being the only heir to the winery, it was decided that I should carry on the name of the oldest brother. I became Camille Roche, the future of Maison Roche.

Being the only heir to a vineyard destined to be outstanding in the Côtes du Rhône was both a joy and a burden. Everyone in the family adored me. No matter where I roamed on the estate, people took the time to explain their jobs and how their efforts contributed to the puzzle that made Maison Roche great. This puzzle was brought together by all who worked on the estate under the vision of Richard Roche. And the staff who worked in the business, whether daily or seasonally, basked in being a part of what Richard Roche had begun. Grand-père was everywhere I went.

By the time I headed off to college to study viticulture and business, I felt the weight of my inheritance. I knew in my heart that I had to make my grand père proud, and Papa too. There wasn't a day that Papa didn't tell me that Maison Roche was destined to be great and that I was the one to see that it happened. I was the one who would outlive Uncle Emile's old ways of thinking. I would carry out Papa's dream for Maison Roche.

I returned from university with many new ideas, and while he was alive, Uncle Emile did his best to implement ideas that fit the expanding family business. Papa, of course, saw more than a family business. He saw a wine empire that covered the world. The difference in their views made working with them challenging. While they were both alive, I did my best to manage the conflicting visions.

When Uncle Emile died, Papa was sure the business would finally become the empire he had dreamed of. All he needed was to nurture his contacts in Germany. According to Papa, the Germans knew how to do business. They would make things happen. They did, well, sort of. We began with a small shipment to East Germany each month. The paperwork and time required to cross from West to East didn't seem justified, but Papa said his friends would make it worthwhile. He told me more than once that they were the only people who ever saw him and his business for what it was worth. They would make it happen.

Not many years later, the Berlin Wall fell, and the two Germanys became one. Papa's friends faltered for a while but eventually got a foothold in the new European economy, and we were able to increase shipments. Things were OK for a while, but now our business has competition from cheaper wines from Italy and Spain, and the profits from sales in Germany don't compare to those from the US.

Camille presses the heels of her hands to her eyes and groans. She needs to focus on the present moment. The Americans cannot be allowed to turn those grapes into wine. Rêves Perdus must remain limited and exclusive, and Maison Roche must continue to be the powerhouse that her father had envisioned. Where the Americans and the grapes at Bonne Vie stand in that equation was yet to be determined.

Americans or not, the villa continues to be a thorn in the side of Maison Roche.

7

❦

French Lessons

DAVE, NOVEMBER 2011

There they are, streaks on the glass, again! Stop, breathe.

Relaxing my shoulders and flexing my fingers, I work to release the tension in my upper body, the tension that grabs me every time I see something that's not "right." I cleaned those windows yesterday; they should be crystalline. The view should be spotless, but no, not even the vinegar and newsprint can fix the problem. If I complain to Wendy, she closes the curtains. She doesn't get it; just because I can't see them doesn't mean they're gone. Why can't she see how the streaks ruin the view? It would be such a perfect view if it weren't for the streaks.

Damn, this being retired is driving me crazy. Who had time to worry about windows with work, errands, and chores? Let's face it, even the beautifully landscaped yard in Virginia was nothing compared to Provence. Besides, I never really "saw" that garden.

Last summer was fun, a retirement celebration in the Provence. Drinking wine, eating real French food. A dream. A dream we just figured we'd wake up from at the end of three months, until that day.

The tires crunching on the gravel, the light streaming through the branches of the garden, and then that bounce when we hit the rut— that was my passage into this new world. Throughout our picnic, the Provincial sirens called to me, and although my stomach churned in that familiar "I'm not in control" way, I had little time to pay attention. My senses were on overload. I could actually feel the sun touching my body like a warm feather as it sifted through the leaves of the olive tree. And the smell of lavender. Wendy had raved about it for weeks, but it wasn't until that day in the garden that the relaxing scent enveloped me and I understood its spell. My anxiety disappeared somewhere between the broken tree limbs and the overgrown garden. Even I could hear the song of the waterless fountain. When we drove out of the estate, having tugged the sign from the gate and tossed it onto the back seat, I knew we would return. I had to return.

My soul yearns to feel that calm again, but the old workhorse that I had been has found me behind these walls. He shakes his harness, disrupting my peace with his call to be useful. If only I could settle into this land of the laissez-faire and enjoy the serenity.

My daily walks into town provide a rhythm and give me a goal to accomplish, even if it's just to be at André's corner table before the sun gets above the tops of the plane trees on the square. Sipping my espresso and watching the sunlight sparkle in the dancing water of the fountain reminds me of the Provençal magic that drew us here.

I'm not the only one with a routine. Twice a week, old Pomme shows up with Chien. Pomme catches up on gossip with André, and I practice my French. Ok, I don't actually speak French, but I am getting better at understanding what's going on. I've listened in on complaints about everything, from the weather to the tourists. The weather is either too hot or too cold, too wet or too dry or not interesting enough to consider. As for tourists, they are either too stingy to spend money in town, or they are spending too much money, and who do they think they are?

"Do they think we'll let rich foreigners buy up our town?"

Just about then, voices drop, and eyes glance my way. But I've managed to look oblivious and so continue to be thought of as harmless.

Just yesterday, I heard that one of the big-box stores is considering building a facility on the outskirts of the community, just off the A7 highway. I must admit, the French do know how to debate a topic. I have heard it all.

"Très bien! It will save people the time of driving into Avignon or Orange for clothes and supplies."

"A store like that will ruin our beautiful countryside!"

"How will Pomme make any money selling his fruit and vegetables with store produce displayed like a painting?"

"Will tourists come through town or just stop at the grocery store?"

"Will the store increase traffic through town and cause a hazard for those of us who walk the narrow country roads?"

"The maire is being bought off by the grocery company. He only cares about making his family richer so that his children can inherit a prosperous mayoral position when it's their turn to be elected."

This is an interesting fact about small-town life in France. The job of mayor is passed down from generation to generation within the same family. From tradition, one could be led to believe that the ability to look after the well-being of a town is a genetic disposition. Or maybe it has to do with the lifelong training mayoral families provide their children in French law and glad-handing. Elections or not, surnames tend to remain the same on town documents from one generation to the next.

Finishing my coffee and croissant, I trudge back to the villa to begin my online French lesson. After we struggled to translate the sign we took from the gate, and had to pay for translators to manage the purchase of the villa, I decided I would learn the language. Where else does an American adult begin to learn French but at a community college? I diligently memorized verb conjugations and spent more than the required two hours a week in the language lab. I even found French movies on YouTube to get into a French mood, hoping my lips would move in proper form. But after two semesters, the only words that pass my lips in public are Bonjour, mon ami. Une tasse de café et un croissant, s'il vous plaît. L'addition, s'il vous plaît. Merci. Passez une bonne journée. I may not say much, but my pronunciation is perfect when I do speak.

Now that I'm out of school, I've signed up for an online language program. I haven't missed a day in almost a year. Wendy grits her teeth each time she hears the electronic tones of an error. I'm pretty sure it's the profanity that follows that bothers her and not the tones themselves. But hey, I'm swearing in two languages now. Anyway, I've learned to do my lessons where she can't hear. It makes for a happier marriage.

I have arranged my mornings with a fine routine, but after lunch, I find myself adrift. It seems everyone else has a purpose, a direction for their days. Lee is working with local builders to update the villa. Wendy is designing a website for the new Bed and Breakfast. Josh spends his days visiting local markets and talking to Pomme about the local produce he'd like for the menus. He wants to provide guests with meals that fit the ambiance of the villa. Me? I'm a retired dentist whose license means nothing in France, even if I did want to work.

Forty years of routine, following rules, and knowing where I belonged in the world have brought me here. Retirement in Provence. Retirement in Eden. I'm lost in Eden. Some days I wonder what my epitaph will be.

David Andrews

Dentist

He followed the rules

I wonder what life is like for people who don't live inside the box that rules create.

I blow on my hands as I rub some warmth into my fingers, raw from my morning walk to André's. So, this is what those famous Mistral winds are all about. Although the day is sunny, it's as though the wind snatches away the rays' warmth before they can reach my body. The French are hardy souls who love to sit side by side outside the cafes, sipping espresso and speaking of life. But today, not even they are braving the cold.

I step into the crowded café, warm and buzzing with life. André's eyes widen as he looks up in greeting. I can't tell if he's surprised to see me or is impressed that I've kept my date. Nodding, he cocks his head towards a small table at the back of the café, crammed with locals.

"Excusez-moi, excusez-moi," I smile and nod as I make my way between the tables. By the time I've taken off my coat and settled in, André is setting my cup of espresso and one of his flaky croissants on the table. "Merci!" I smile up at him in appreciation. Sometimes, being a man of habit pays off.

Time to tune into today's episode of "Village Life in Provence." What is the question du jour? I know I really should speak more French, but my perceived ignorance of the language has opened a voyeuristic door I am hesitant to shut. A few months ago, the decision to locate the big box store further down the A7 was announced, and conversation settled back into the more mundane. Have you seen Luca's new car? Has Chloė returned from her visit to her mother? Do you think Pomme is up to truffle season this year?

What are we talking about today?

"He's here again today."

"Even with the Mistral."

"I was sure they would leave at the end of the season."

"No, they have hired Gérard to plumb four new bathrooms."

"Do they each need their own bathroom? Can't Americans share a bathroom?"

Ah, WE are the question du jour.

"All the changes to the villa worry me. I'm afraid they will drive the magic away."

The room grows quiet, and people look down as if in silent prayer.

Magic? What magic? I think.

"The magic remained after Monsieur left us."

"Yes, but Madame was still here."

"I was worried when she passed away, but I could still feel something when I visited Pomme."

"These days things feel different."

"Yes, but Fabian says he can still feel it."

"Fabian's just happy to spend time with Madame's cat again."

"No, Pomme says he feels it too."

Once again, the table quiets as everyone looks for comfort at the bottom of their coffee cup.

"But without Monsieur or Madame…"

"This one," the speaker cocks his head my way, "has Monsieur's ways. He walks to André's every morning."

"He's quiet, just as Monsieur was."

"But does he understand what's going on?"

"Monsieur always knew where to lay his hand."

"Half of us wouldn't be here if it weren't for Monsieur." Heads turn as they take in the room, nodding as their eyes land on various neighbors.

"The magic must continue." A silent agreement unites the group.

Then, sadly, someone whispers, "But he's an American! How could he possibly make a difference here?"

People around me silently pay their bills, tightly wrapping their scarves about them as they head to the door, leaving me with a partially eaten croissant and too many questions.

Monsieur, this benevolent specter whose shadow we've been living under, was more than just the owner of the villa. He was an important figure in the village who was sorely missed. He made a difference in people's lives. Now that's a legacy.

He knew where to make a difference. Unlike me. I've always been one to walk the well-trodden path, one foot before the other, staying within the lines. How can I make a difference for other people?

As I ruminate on my lack of legacy, a niggling thought pokes at me. Magic. There was a magic about Monsieur. But they say they can still feel it.

Memories of our first visit to the garden flood in. The spell of the lavender, the warmth of the sun, and … the magic. Maybe it wasn't Monsieur. Maybe it's the villa, the space inside the walls.

Can I find the magic? And when I do, what do I do with it?

8

The Habanera Effect

GÉRARD, DECEMBER 2011

MAIS SI JE T'AIME, SI JE T'AIME, PRENDS GARDE À TOI !, THE LYRICS from La Habanera swirl in my mind. Shining the sink fixtures, I step back to take in the bathroom and let the words remind me that I've completed yet another job. How many years has it been now? I was just an apprentice the first time I heard those words. The soprano at the Théâtre Antique d'Orange was singing La Habanera as I finished rebuilding la toilette all those years ago. That day, Albert left me to guard the toilette he had disassembled while he went in search of parts. I passed the time listening to the cast practice Bizet's Carmen. By the time he returned from the plumbing store, and God knows where else, I could sing "Votre toast, je peux vous le rendre" as though I were the toreador. Then, as I reassembled la toilette, I sang along with Carmen just to drive Albert crazy. That time I sang to irritate my hapless boss, but since then the song has become a part of my routine. My wife calls it the Habanera Effect.

Sunlight glinting from the mirror above the sink brings my thoughts back to the villa. I gaze at the fountain below where Le Chat finishes drinking and gently curls into a black ball of fur in a warming patch of sun. The Mistral, known for freezing the sun's rays, has taken a vacation on this crisp December day. Taking advantage of the beautiful weather, the villa's new occupants have gone to Sète in hopes of finding a fishmonger for Josh to work with and a lunch fresh from the sea.

The trip to the coast is meant to raise everyone's spirits as the occupants are about to spend their first Christmas in France, away from family. The addition of the four new bathrooms and modernization of the existing plumbing have gone smoothly and rather quickly by French standards—standards that usually include delayed starts, suspended efforts mid-project, and finishing touches that take months to come to fruition. Being the former home of Monsieur and Madame, just the mention of the job's location brought contractors in an unusually speedy manner. Whether it was curiosity or the magic of the place, no one can be sure.

Quick responses or not, the web of plumbing in the walls and the intricate flow to and from the bathrooms have left the group with alternating toilet and bathing options. For months, they have been bathing vagabonds shifting from bathroom to bathroom, from the old servants' quarters on the second floor all the way out to the new bathing facilities in the garden shed. For Americans, they have done well to share the shifting accommodations. It was the lack of adequate plumbing that required the family's first visit to be rescheduled. Instead of Christmas, the family will have to wait until March to share their new French adventure.

In the quiet house, my mind has space to wander. From here, I watch the dancing water, flashes of sunlight reflect from droplets as they tumble back to the azure basin, only to be lifted once more; liquid prisms splitting the light into tiny rainbows. Hypnotized, I am taken back to the day I first saw the fountain.

"No, you can't put that rusty old faucet on the new pipes."

"The old fool will never know, he never comes to the shed, and Fabian's just a stupid lapdog, he'll never say a thing."

"But Albert, you've charged Monsieur a lot of money, and it's not a difficult job. The least you could do is give him new fixtures."

"You think you've learned it all, eh boy? After today, you may not be my apprentice anymore, but today I'm still the master."

"Then you do the job, because I won't!"

Wrapped in frustration, I stomped away.

It hadn't taken long for me to realize how ill-matched my mentor and I were, but everyone had assured me Albert would teach me how to be a plumber. Being curious and having taken apart everything Maman would allow, I already knew quite a bit about pipes, water pressure, and valves. My teachers were dismayed when I didn't continue my education at university, but I wanted a profession that allowed me to be curious and solve problems. Besides, I'm not cut out for doing the same job day after day. My mind needs challenges.

I did learn many lessons from Albert. Most importantly, I learned how not to run a business. Albert tumbled out of bed each morning, arriving rumpled and smelly, his clothes a palette of his last meal and his breath an odd mix of garlic and pastis. His truck, caked in Provincial dirt, would squeal to a stop in front of the shop where I waited to begin the workday. Albert's sense of time was lousy, even for a Frenchman. His poor hygiene and tardiness were just a few signs of his lack of attention to detail. The mess Albert left in his wake grated on me constantly.

I have always preferred things to be neat and organized. Maman used to talk about how other mothers complained about their children's messes. She would shake her head. My toys were always lined up neatly. I put my clothes in the drawers or hung them on the pegs in my room. One day, I scared Papa when he found me balancing between the toilet and sink to wash my hands. That's when he built a wooden box for me to use.

It took me a long time before I understood what he meant when he said, "Another gift those damn Germans left behind." It turns out that the family rumor is that Grand-mère fell in love with a wounded soldier the family had been required to house during the war. The soldier succumbed to his wounds and Grand-mère married soon afterward, but Maman's blond hair and blue eyes left the town something to talk about. As soon as she was old enough, Maman apprenticed to a dressmaker in Toulouse to escape the small-town gossip. She met Papa on holiday and happily left the family history behind.

Back in the villa, my grumbling stomach tells me it's time for lunch. I find a sunny spot in the garden and settle in next to a wall that has been warmed by the sun. It doesn't take long before Le Chat is rubbing against my leg. After appreciating the tokens of my lunch, Le Chat settles in at my side. The sparkling fountain, a warming sun, and a purring cat carry my memory back to the week after my apprenticeship ended.

Sitting at a table in André's café, I perused the help wanted ads in the Avignon edition of Le Monde. I had begun my job hunt before finishing my apprenticeship, but it seemed that every interview stalled as soon as they heard Albert's name. Albert's reputation mattered more than what I could do. Had I really wasted four years learning to be a plumber just to find a job as a dishwasher in some tourist spot in Avignon?

A shadow fell across my newspaper. I looked up to find André standing above me. "Monsieur would like you to visit the villa. He asked that you bring your tools."

"Me? He wants to see me?"

André nodded.

"Why me?"

"I didn't ask." André shrugged and walked away.

I left money for *l'addition* and headed home to pick up my tools. My tools, were they another waste? "A loan to pay for tools that I'll never use, and no way to pay for them. Washing dishes won't even get me enough to make that payment, much less buy a ring for Lili" I fretted. I was so wrapped up in self-pity that it took a while for me to wonder why I had been called back to the villa. Had that rusty faucet given way already? That was Albert's doing. Monsieur should be calling Albert, not me. But I knew what Albert did, and I didn't say anything. It's only right that I take care of it.

The cook answered my knock on the kitchen door. "Un instant, s'il vous plaît."

I took in the dancing water of the fountain as I waited. I recalled the week before, when Madame sat before the waterworks and marveled at how much higher the water rose after the new pipes had been installed. She and Le Chat had enjoyed the water show from the shade of the trellis.

The cook returned, "Monsieur asks that you see Fabian. I think he is in the garden shed."

The garden shed, where the rusty faucet is. "Merci!" I headed for the shed.

"Bonjour!" I called out as I entered. Fabian was busy cutting wires for the grape arbor, preparing the additional supports the vines would need as the grapes grew heavier.

"Ah, Gérard, you have come." Picking up a shiny new faucet, he handed it to me. "Monsieur would like you to install this in place of the rusty one." Fabien inclined his head towards the piping and faucet that had been installed the week before. I could feel my face redden with embarrassment and looked away. I reached out to take the faucet, but Fabien held tight until I looked up. "The Monsieur knows the truth. He misses very little." I nodded and took the faucet.

Mais si je t'aime, si je t'aime, prends garde à toi!, the music bounced around my brain, and I smiled to myself, another job complete. I felt better knowing that the new faucet was installed. I had no intention of asking to be paid. I knew the job should have been done right the first time. In fact, the knot that I'd had in my stomach when I arrived was gone. It felt good to have the opportunity to make amends. When I turned to leave, I noticed Monsieur standing in the doorway. I wondered how long he'd been there.

"Thank you for your thorough work," Monsieur said, handing me an envelope.

"Thank you, Monsieur, but I can't take payment for something that should have been done correctly the first time."

"Your honor is appreciated and is the reason I have asked you to return. You have completed the work I requested today, so you have earned this compensation. In the envelope, you will also find a letter of introduction to Monsieur Lyon at the Hotel Deveria. He is in need of a house plumber and handyman. The position requires a person of honor who can be trusted to service rooms while they are occupied. I have assured him you are that person."

Struck mute with surprise, I nodded my head and took the envelope. As I passed, I was scarcely able to mumble a soft, "*Merci*, Monsieur."

Working in a hotel hadn't been what I had in mind when I chose a career in plumbing. I had visions of owning my own business and being an important part of the community, someone people could count on. This might not be my dream, but it would allow me to make my loan payments and consider a future with Lili. Patting the letter in my pocket, I was thankful for Monsieur's generosity.

I became the first in-house plumber the hotel had ever had. The patch-the-leaks-and-keep-marching attitude of the previous manager had left a jumbled maze of poorly connected pipes, causing problems almost daily, which was the exact reason an in-house plumber had become necessary.

I spent my first year on the property learning about the state of the building and convincing management that they would be better served by updating the pipes than continuing the old patch-the-leak policy. I finally gained the manager's confidence and was able to use each new leak as an opportunity to gradually replace the building's decaying water pipes with new copper ones. Over time, most of the lines had been replaced, and problems dwindled. Not a person to sit idle, I found new ways to help. There were days I sat with the assistant manager while he agonized over the schedule. Other days, I answered phones for the front desk, sorted invoices, and posted checks for the bookkeeper. I even helped in the laundry, though to be honest, that exploit began with a call to fix a washing machine.

During my last spring at the hotel, an unknown virus spread among the staff. Being the kid who graduated from school with perfect attendance, I took the newest flu in stride. Whether this was another gift of my rumored German heritage or not, I arrived at the hotel every day ready to work wherever I was needed. I happily manned the front desk, updated the shifting schedule, served as the maître d' for the restaurant, and carted suitcases to and from rooms. My work made an impression on the manager, and a week after the staff had returned to health, Monsieur Lyon called me to his office.

Sitting behind the heavy, ornately carved desk from which he steered the hotel, M. Lyon commanded respect. Always precisely dressed in his custom-made gray suit, kerchief exactly 5 centimeters above the lapel pocket, a Napoleon knot in his cravate, and perfectly manicured nails, he oozed self-assured aloofness. In the five years that I had worked at the hotel, we had spoken little. M. Lyon preferred to communicate via his assistant manager, unless, of course, you were a guest of utmost quality and standing for whom he would deign to extend a hand in greeting and inquire as to your preferences.

"Gérard, your work over the last month has been more than we could have imagined. We knew you were an excellent plumber and handyman, but we had no idea how efficiently you could handle hotel business. The reviews from our guests have been excellent. We would like to invite you to join our management program here at Hôtel Deveria. We will train you in all areas of hotelier and one day you may work your way into a position of great stature."

I was astounded by the compliment. "Thank you, M. Lyon. I'm blown away by the offer, but I really like being a plumber. I've had a great time here. I got to replumb the whole place and learn some business stuff too. Now that I've updated the place, there's not much for me to do these days. I think I should look for something new. Thanks, though."

"Yes, it does look as though you have worked yourself out of a job as our plumber. Should you change your mind about management, you are always welcome."

I was proud of the work I'd done at the hotel, but I'd known for a while that it was time to move on. My studies for the master plumber test were going well, and I found out I had been granted a seat at the testing center for the next exam. Once I had my certificate, I would be a master plumber. It was time to consider what to do next.

Whistling the tune from La Habanera, I bounced down the steps from the manager's office and reflected on the past five years. The income from the hotel had allowed me to pay off my tools and purchase a ring for Lili. Last summer, we were married and moved into a small apartment. Once I fixed the knocking pipes and put things in place, we were happy in our nest.

A week after the exam, I sat at a table on André's patio watching the sunlight flash from the water of the fountain in the square, enjoying the unique song of the falling drops.

André appeared at the table. "I don't see you much anymore. Seems you only come by when Lili's aunt is sick."

"Yeah, Aunt Marie seems to ail when she doesn't see enough of Lili. But seeing me isn't part of the deal." I chuckle. "That's OK, I'd rather drink your coffee than her tea."

"Have you heard? Albert wants to retire. The apprentice he took on, after you, didn't work out, and he's tired of working. His business is for sale." André raised his eyebrow in a questioning manner and returned to his duties.

What business? The old warehouse space probably hadn't been touched since I left. Was that old truck still running? Albert does have a business name and a phone number, though. And most importantly, it's already registered in the National Trades and Crafts Register. Albert is the only plumber here in L'Esprit du Rhône. However, when they can, people try to wait for the plumber from Orange or one of the guys from Avignon. I bet I could change that. If there were a reliable plumber who provided good service, people wouldn't have to wait. Would there be enough work to support Lili and me, as well as the family we want to have? A multitude of questions cascaded through my mind. Buying a business would require money. Money, we don't have. No house and almost no savings. Who would even consider giving me a loan?

My attention returned to the fountain as I thought - the song of the fountain mixed with my memory of Madame's laughter. Not knowing exactly why, I tossed money on the table and walked towards the bank. I could ask about the business. I'm sure the bank will have information on the sale.

Monsieur De la Cour sat calmly behind his desk, nodding as I looked for words to express my interest in my former mentor's business. When I stopped speaking, he answered.

"Yes, we have the particulars on Albert's business. In fact, this bank holds the note for the enterprise. Albert needs to sell it in order to retire. I'm sure we can work out an arrangement."

"I really want my own business. I know I'm good at it, and people will like my work. The trouble is, M. De La Cour, I don't have any collateral."

"Your signature is good with us, and of course, the business will remain in the name of the bank until you have finished paying the note."

"Really? I, I can't believe this. Of course, I'll pay off the note," I gulped. "This is too good to be true. How? Why?"

"Your honor precedes you, Gérard. At this bank, you are known as a man of his word."

Stepping out into the sun, I squinted and became vividly present. I looked at the papers in my hand to reassure myself I wasn't dreaming. I had ten days to review the business and make a decision. Money would be tight for a while, but once word got out that I had taken over Albert's business, people would call me instead of waiting for a plumber from Orange or Avignon. I knew people would trust me. If the bank would trust me with a loan, surely people would trust me with their plumbing. And Lili? Yes, she would support my decision.

My decision? Had I really made a decision? A few weeks before, I had told M. Lyon I would be looking for a new position, and today I am beginning my own business. It all happened so fast. André sharing Albert's retirement. The bank approving a loan. Everything just fell into place. I couldn't put my finger on it, but I had the feeling something else was going on. Whatever it was, I was grateful.

My lunch long finished, I notice the sun has shifted, and the chilling of the air reminds me it's time to get back to work. Tomorrow I will begin the last two bathrooms, and I'd like to move the fixtures into the house while everyone is away.

"Come on, Chat, the sun has moved, and so must we. Off to your warm spot on the other side of the house." Chat arches its back and rubs against me as I clear away my lunch. When it is time for Chat to leave this garden for a celestial one, I wonder if another one will wander in to take her place, as has been the case since Madame adopted her first furry friend. Rubbing Chat behind the ears, I feel a calm joy. It is the feeling this place has given me since I replaced that old faucet. It's the feeling the community had feared was lost.

But life has returned to the villa, and the enchantment continues.

9

La Cornue

JOSH, JANUARY 2012

THE VIBRATION OF THE SLAMMING DOOR HITS MY BODY.
Damn, I hope his tantrum doesn't cause the soufflé to fall. I've finally perfected the ratio of eggplant to cheese and don't need his insecurities ruining lunch.

Slamming doors are nothing new to my relationship with Lee. When he's feeling anxious, logic and reason are useless. Somewhere in his brain, a switch goes off, and his ability to hear or use words disappears. He stomps, slams doors, and has even been known to growl a bit.

Ah, I remember the first time I heard him growl. Soon after we began dating, Lee took me to a trendy watering hole in DC. After a few glasses of Light My Fire, great name for a house special, I was feeling loose and happy. So happy that I forgot myself and smiled at everyone. This might sound innocent enough, but smiling is my superpower. Turning on what Lee calls my thousand-watt beacon draws in men and women of all ages. I first realized its power in high school when I used it to convince Mrs. Vance, my physics teacher, to curve a less-than-stellar grade into something more in line with my other grades. While everyone else was practicing cool pick-up lines, I was brushing my pearly whites and grinning in the mirror. The gift was handy when I ran the front of the house for Chef Robert. An understanding look and appreciative smile, with a wink at the wife, and a disgruntled guest was more than happy to accept a table near the kitchen.

That evening in DC was like a revolving door. Just as I'd fend off one well-wisher, another would arrive. After the third person, a low purr began to emanate from Lee. By the time I had sidestepped the fifth person and pulled Lee from the bar, he was in full growl. Stomping down the street, he left me looking for a full moon and second-guessing all I knew about werewolves. Since then, I've learned to read the signs of his discomfort and avoid public displays of his jealousy.

Four, three, two, one—time's up! Fluffy soufflé, here we come. Brown and crusty on the outside. The savory steam was causing my mouth to water. I can almost taste the rich, creamy texture.

The La Cornue technician was right. If the oven is calibrated correctly, I can trust the timer. Old man Dupuy knew what he was doing when he created that vaulted oven. But I miss the Zen state I get while watching my creations bake.

This soufflé, like the others, is perfect, just as the baking guide said it would be. "Trust the magic of the oven." Every time I read that line, I see Keebler elves baking in trees. I'd like to believe whoever wrote La Cornue manuals in the '60s was the inspiration for the Keebler cookie commercials of the '80s.

Time to call the gang together for lunch. I'm surprised no one has stuck their head in to find out when we'll eat. Ah, yes, Lee's tantrum. His stomping off set up a no-go zone for everyone else, even with the magical smells tickling their noses. Oh, Lee and his jealousy.

Jealousy is never a good thing, so it took me a while to allow myself to fall in love with Lee. He was hard to avoid, though, as he was the design architect that Chef Robert had chosen to remodel Un Peu de France. Lee was known as the man to call in the DC area if you wanted to add a French touch to your décor. Chef Robert had interviewed a few other interior architects before deciding he would wait for the very busy Lee to be available.

Robert was immediately enchanted with the man who spoke his language and loved his food. It took me longer to engage with this man, who seemed to have mastered the French effect of superiority. Chef Robert had his own ideas of style, but I was adamant that the restaurant's flow was crucial for both the guests and the staff. I spent one Sunday afternoon walking Lee through the theater that was the experience of dining at Un Peu de France and demanded that he participate in a Saturday night production before laying pencil to paper.

By the end of the evening, Lee thoroughly understood my vision and the importance of the flow to the dining performance. During the month that it took to transform the dining room, I found myself trailing Lee as he managed the movement of walls, electrical supply, and lighting & sound systems, followed by the installation of the perfect flooring and ceiling tiles. Lee was attentive to every step of the process, determined to give me the stage on which to present Chef Robert's creations.

"The dining room is perfect! What a team the two of you make. Josh, please assure me I won't lose you to the restaurant design business. I can't imagine Peu de France without its maestro. No one conducts a dining experience like you!"

I prized these words of praise. It had taken five years for me to earn this distinction. Something I couldn't have dreamed of as my entry to the restaurant business had not been the usual.

Food has always been my passion. While the rest of my buddies were eating cheap hamburgers at the local dive, I was at home convincing my mother of the value of fresh, ground prime beef over plastic-wrapped chuck on a Styrofoam tray. From an early age, I had been describing and critiquing her meals. It began at age five with -

"Tonight, Mom made meatballs on top of a hill of spaghetti covered in tomato sauce and sprinkled with cheese."

As my vocabulary grew and I increased my viewing of cooking shows, my announcements became more sophisticated.

"Tonight, chef Rebecca brings us a delectable bed of al dente linguini embracing two exquisitely spiced meatballs of freshly ground prime beef bathed in an Italian red gravy redolent with garlic and basil, finished with generous shavings of finely aged parmesan cheese."

What had begun as cute became a tolerated family tradition, that is, until I started scoring the meals as well. After a week of ratings that didn't rise above a 6, Chef Rebecca decided it was time for a new chef to take over the kitchen. So, I did! After a grocery list that included caviar, double English cream, Canadian bacon, and kiwi (this was the 70's, mind you), I was informed that I would have to cook from what the now sous-chef, Rebecca, stocked the kitchen with. To her credit, she did bring home at least one new or unusual food each week, and I could request an ingredient as long as it didn't break the bank.

My gift with words led me to join the journalism club and work on the school newspaper. I don't know many high school papers that regularly contain reviews of local hangouts, but in our town, kids knew where to find the best deep-dish pizza, the chewiest crust, or a crackly thin crust. Spoiler alert, they couldn't be found in the same restaurant.

When it was time for college, I considered the CIA (Culinary Institute of America) and Johnson and Wales, but my second and third loves, writing and baseball, teamed up to pull me away. A baseball scholarship, along with a handful of journalism grants, hit a home run with my parents, pun intended.

The four years at James Madison University flew by. Of course, spring semesters were filled with baseball strategy, strengthening, sportsmanship, and drills. From January to May, I barely had time to complete the required classwork. On game days, attendance at afternoon classes wasn't expected, and on away game days, we reported to the bus after our first-period class. My only time to consider food was the sick feeling in my stomach as I gathered up empty fast-food wrappers from burgers I had just devoured. A ravenous appetite tends to dull one's senses, only to end in regret once the hunger has subsided. But I did love baseball. I loved being a Duke, being part of a team, and working my muscles. In the first few years, I thought I might follow my joy into the big leagues. But a scout who visited the game with Roanoke at the end of my sophomore year disabused me of that idea.

But in the fall, oh in the fall when the chill hits the air, the leaves crunch and it's time to enjoy the summer's harvest, I'm all about writing—writing about food to be exact. In college, I expanded the restaurant review style I had developed in high school. During my freshman year, I began with the student joints in town. But it was my Thanksgiving review of The Old House that got everyone's attention. Everyone knew The Old House was the place your parents took you when they visited, but no one thought much about what they were eating, and The Old House banked on it. By the time the owner obtained that November edition, tongues were wagging. No one had dared to lay it out so clearly.

Resting on their laurels… dining room in need of not only a cleaning, but a past due makeover… overcooked vegetables, a sad choice in a state bursting with tasty fall produce…but don't fire the pastry chef, the maple cheesecake with its unique cinnamon apple compote made the evening worthwhile.

My review made a big splash, and I was the one who ended up covered in mud. At a friendly meeting with the dean, I was advised to take my talents beyond the University's donor base. Thankfully, baseball began after the holiday break, so I had a few months to find a new direction for my reviews.

Harrisonburg is a mere two and a half hours from Washington D.C., and the ride is even shorter for places like Manassas, Fairfax, Tysons Corner, and Alexandria. The fall of my junior year, after a quick update on the local pizza and burger scene, I headed east. I had to argue with the editor of The Breeze to get my work published, but after President Andrews commented to Professor Lane, the head of the journalism department, about the excellent meal he'd had at a restaurant I'd suggested, my reviews found a regular space in the culture section.

As more people made culinary forays to the east, I began receiving invitations from restaurants eager to attract new diners. Being the cocky 20-year-old that I was, I took the free meals and wrote my reviews with little thought of the consequences. Then came the angry restaurant owner who didn't get the review he had "paid for." And the other restaurateurs who felt my column provided unfair coverage to those unwilling to pay for a review. By the end of the semester, I found myself avoiding the hot spots. I even took to wearing disguises lest I be recognized. Thank goodness for baseball in the spring. My column went on hiatus, and my name fell from the lips of the dining crowd.

That spring was not a good season for The Dukes. We didn't even make it to the playoffs, so things wound down early. A disappointing season and too much takeout put me in the mood for comfort food. By comfort food, I mean finely prepared and artfully presented fresh food. It was my search for such a meal that led me to cruise the Alexandria area on a Saturday night that spring.

I arrived early and slid into the small two-top just outside the kitchen. This is an excellent place for someone like me. As the door to the kitchen opens and closes, I can hear the waiters reporting to the kitchen crew on how the dishes were received. I can also hear the kitchen staff's response to the diner's feedback. Where the kitchen meets the front of the house is where you feel the heartbeat of an operation.

As the dining room filled, traffic in front of my table increased. The buzz filled me with joy. The kitchen hummed like clockwork without being mechanical. Waitstaff and sous-chefs bantered helpfully while the dining room remained calm, but not dead. I had found a true jewel and wasn't sure I wanted to share it with anyone.

As I surreptitiously jotted a few notes in my notebook, a shadow fell across my table.

"You have any suggestions you'd like to share with us?"

"Ah, no. Well…maybe." As much as I was enjoying myself, I had noticed a few areas that could use tweaking.

"I've been watching you watching us. Not many diners want to sit near the kitchen. But for you, it's like dinner and a show."

"You might call it that." I'd never thought of it that way, but he was right. As much as I love good food, well-choreographed service can make or break the evening.

"Would you consider watching the show from the bar? We have a reservation waiting. When I told them you could have the table at 7:00 pm I didn't think it would screw with our reservations."

"Sorry about messing up your reservation book. I can do the bar."

If you're still here when things slow down, I'll buy you a drink and listen to your suggestions."

With a wave of his hand, the choreography altered slightly. The show swooped past my table, carrying me and my dishes to a cozy place at the far end of the bar.

That night opened the door to my career in fine dining. Robert asked me to work in the kitchen for the summer—a job I came to realize did not fit my talents or temperament. Clanking cookware, repetitious movements that produce picture-perfect plating, and a dance that takes years to perfect did not endear me to the job.

On my last day that summer, Robert called me to his office. My smile and can-do attitude did little to hide the knot in my stomach and an invisible hand squeezing my heart.

"Look, Josh. You're a good kid. You know what tastes good. You know what looks good. You have good restaurant sense, but you are NOT a chef."

There it was: the truth. I had known it for a while, but didn't want to admit it. I swallowed hard as I fought back tears. How can something feel so right and yet be so wrong?

"I know you're going back to school next week. Would you consider helping out in the front of the house on Fridays and Saturdays? You can help Léon with reservations, fill the easy drink orders at the bar, and keep an eye on the tables. An extra set of hands will lighten everyone's load. Besides, that smile of yours is going to waste out back."

Redemption! Hallelujah! I pumped Robert's hand. "Yes, yes, yes! I would love to help on weekends. Thank you!" I left the restaurant with a song on my lips and a dance in my step. Life was going my way.

Heat radiating through the dish towel burns my fingers and brings me back to the kitchen in Provence. Carefully, I place the soufflé on the serving tray next to the salad and head towards the dining room. As I turn to push the door open with my hip, I appraise the stove.

How can Lee not see how special the oven is to me? I know he thinks the La Cornue has taken his place in my heart, but how could I not love this beautifully crafted wonder? The sturdy form stands erect. I melt each time its heat spreads through me, leaving me in sweaty anticipation. Strong iron bands hold the smooth, glistening exterior together. All of this is specifically designed to meet my needs. I love my oven.

Hmm. Maybe Lee has a point.

Turning to walk through the butler's pantry, I am once again assailed by the perfection of this dish. I may not be able to smell the eggplant over the cheese, but I know the taste of the purple orb I froze in August has blended perfectly with the cheese. We've eaten a myriad of soufflés to get to this scrumptious place, and it's been worth every bite. The mix of textures, crusty exterior, and creamy interior, *merveilleux*!

I have listened to complaints about the stacks of frozen eggplant in the freezer for months. Just once, it would be nice to hear, "You were right, Josh, freezing the eggplant last August was a good idea." They say revenge is sweet, but mine is a creamy soufflé in the middle of January.

January in France is cold. I know it's almost 40 degrees Fahrenheit outside, but the thermometer reads 4 degrees Celsius. Seeing the temperature in Celsius while the heat sucking wind assaults my body makes my mind shout, "It's 4 degrees! It's 4 degrees! To hell with whether it's Fahrenheit or Celsius. It's 4 degrees!"

On days like this, the only place I want to be is in front of my La Cornue. This morning, I made coffee cake from my grandmother's recipe and baked bread while a pot of chicken bones and veggies simmered on the back of the stove. While the soufflé baked, I strained the golden stock from the pot. Everything was humming along. I felt like a cook from a Disney movie where every pot happily sings on an animated stove. How fortunate were we to purchase a house with a La Cornue?

Before we could use the stove, a technician from Paris had to be requested. I spent two days looking over Jacques' shoulder. His thoroughness impressed me. Before reconnecting the gas, he ensured the lines were free of debris, cleaned each burner, adjusted the legs, and tested the seal of the oven door. Finally, he calibrated the thermostat. Jacques was emphatic about the importance of the perfect seal. He says the seal is as vital as the vaulted shape of the baking space.

Throughout the process, he marveled at what an exceptional stove we had. He said repeatedly, "Quel four exceptionnel!" Jacques has been working for La Cornue for 15 years and was one of their top technicians. He had been preparing for a different job in Lyon when he got a call telling him to come to Provence instead. Between his broken English and my poor French, he made me feel like we were in possession of a lost treasure.

"Who is monsieur who buy oven?"

"His name was Arnoux Chalon-Arlay. I think he was a big deal around here. We hear stories about him all the time."

"Oh la la, the house of Orange! Now know why file say take care of monsieur and stove. Stove sent 1964. Vieil homme Dupuy make sure oven built right. This oven Le Château - first year company make it."

"House of Orange? Didn't I read something about them when we visited the Théâtre Antique d'Orange? Weren't they royalty or something?"

"France no have royalty anymore. But monsieur from old family."

"I wonder how someone with royal blood ended up living way out here."

"He love woman. Woman love her home. Man move to be with woman. This no secret."

I laughed because, of course, Jacques could well be right. Our perfect baking machine could be part of an old love story. And it's all mine to enjoy. Except for the days Wendy cooks. During the summer, the give and take was easier, as I spent a lot of time with Pomme in his garden. And when the heat of summer set in, no one wanted to be in a hot kitchen anyway. Most days, we "made do" with a fresh salad, cheese and charcuterie, a cold bottle of rosé, and crusty baguettes from the bakery.

Now that it's cold, we spend little time outside, and both of us are subject to the siren song of our La Cornue. After a few days of bumping elbows and arguing about how to prepare dishes, we agreed to disagree and came to an arrangement, at least till the weather improves. I cook on Mondays, Wednesdays, and Fridays. She cooks on Tuesday, Thursday, and Saturday, and we alternate Sundays.

This has solved the time issue, but her laissez-faire kitchen arrangements still drive me crazy. Just last week, I reached for a whisk and came up with a gaudy pink spatula. What was that outrageous tool doing with my stainless utensils? It took everything I had not to scream or to throw the damned thing in the trash. Right now, it's well hidden in the back of the wrappings drawer. As for the pots and pans, we've agreed that I will wash them, and none of the enameled cast-iron ovenware is to be put in the dishwasher. Luckily, Dave supports me on this. As Wendy's sous chef, he's always been stuck with the clean-up. My need to clean the cookware "properly" only makes his life easier.

We have called a truce, and I will abide by our agreement, for now. Come spring, I'll be back in the garden with Pomme. We have plans! Last summer, I got so excited walking through his neatly formed rows of eggplant, zucchini, peppers, onions, and radishes. Oh, those radishes. What is it about the French soil that grows such crisp and tasty root vegetables? Breakfast radishes? I thought that was just a name, not something you actually ate for breakfast. But heaven knows, they are a perfect accompaniment to eggs and toast or next to one of the ham and cheese croissants from Jules's patisserie.

Poor Pomme, I think I overwhelmed the old guy. I got so excited about serving vegetables fresh from the garden he felt the need to add more rows of plants after the season had begun. Mind you, it didn't take much to inspire him, but it's been a few years since he's taken on such a large project.

He gave us quite a start last July. I was out walking the garden in search of the perfect tomatoes for my French tart when Chien's frantic barking sent me in a different direction.

As I came up over the rise, Chien's barking and bouncing up and down increased. I looked around for Pomme, knowing the two are rarely far apart. I was nearly on top of Pomme's crumpled body before I saw him. If it hadn't been for Chien, I don't know how long it would have taken us to find the old gardener. As I knelt next to Pomme, Chien's yelping changed to a soft growl, his eyes watching my every move.

"It's OK, boy, I'm here to help."

Luckily, I was able to rouse Pomme, then half supporting and half dragging the burly old man, we managed to stumble back to his house. A little water and time in the shade brought him around.

"Pomme, what happened?"

"I pick giant." A giant is what we'd come to call zucchini that hide under the leaves and avoid being picked until they are huge.

"We need to get you to the doctor."

"Je vais bien. Je suis juste chaud."

Shaking my head, I moved to the phone and called Lee. Pomme protested. He had no use for doctors, but with Lee's smooth French and my smiling, we convinced Pomme to make the visit.

What Lee was able to make out from the conversation with the doctor was that, after his breakfast coffee, Pomme had headed to the garden. He'd been so involved in his gardening and dreams of more plants that he didn't think to stop to eat or drink anything. Low blood sugar, dehydration, and bending over to pick a giant zucchini culminated in him being prone in the garden.

"Voyez, je suis en bonne forme. Je retourne dans mon jardin."

"He says he's in good shape and he's going back to his garden."

"Oui, mais vous restez quand même humain. Vous avez besoin de manger et de boire de l'eau. Et de vous reposer!"

"The doctor told him he's still human, so he needs to eat and drink. And also rest!"

"Lee, this is my fault. Pomme is healthy for a guy in his 80s, but he can't do all of that work by himself. We need to get him some help."

Even before Lee could translate Pomme's response, I knew he wasn't happy. He didn't trust anyone to treat his land with the love that he did. The old man had taught his children and his wife "the right way" to work the land. He was too old to bother teaching anyone new. We could tell this was going to be a battle, so we retreated from the argument until another day.

Dave returned from André's the next day, saying the topic of the day was how the Americans had pushed Pomme too hard. What were they thinking, pushing an old man that way? Just let him tend to his few rows of vegetables and enjoy his old age.

That didn't last long, though. Once Pomme got wind of it, he let it be known that he wasn't ready to give up yet and was happy that someone valued him and his garden. That's when André stepped in with the solution, Margot.

Margot was a bright local girl with designs on university. She loved nature and wanted to become a botanist. She had spent years caring for her mother's and grandmother's gardens and experimenting with ways to improve the harvest from their small patches of vegetables. Last summer, she took a job at a local nursery but was not happy. She wanted to grow things. Plant them, nurture them, and harvest the fruits of her labor. She wanted to connect with the land to bring out the best it had to offer, not grow pretty pots to decorate the windows of lazy summer gardeners.

It took Pomme a while to warm up to the idea of having help, much less from a girl. At first, he made her watch him work. Then he watched her work. When she did anything different from the way Pomme wanted it done, there was a lot of shouting. Those were the days Chien had to referee. Standing between them, Chien would lean against Pomme's legs until he could compose himself. The impasse continued until the day Pomme went searching for Chien. Coming over a hill, he found Margot and Chien settled next to a potato plant.

"See this green squishy thing right here? That's a potato worm. It will make great bait for my brother when he fishes in the Rhône, but this worm is no good for our pretty potato plant, so it goes in the can." Chien's nose followed Margot's hand as she deposited the worm in the can. "Some people are lazy and spread that white powder everywhere. But we know better. If we use the powder, you won't have any *papillon* to chase. And what would summer be without you dancing with those flitting spots of color?"

Pomme realized that Margot loved the land as much as he did, and though he hated to admit it, she did have a few good ideas. From that day on, Pomme and Margot worked in harmony. This freed up Chien to chase butterflies once again. At the end of the summer, Margot was off to university with a promise to return in the spring when it was time to plant the new garden. Together they would tend the garden through the summer and celebrate the harvest. Until then, my supply of local produce would come from the jars of sauces and preserves in the cellar or the chest freezer.

By the end of lunch, Lee had come to his senses. Realizing an apology was in order, he helped clear the table and kept me company in the kitchen while I cleaned up. In the first few months we lived together, Lee tried to help with kitchen chores, but after reorganizing the dishwasher for the umpteenth time, I had to set some ground rules. The kitchen is my domain. I need it to be just the way I need it to be. If this means I do all of the work in the kitchen, so be it. Working in the kitchen had never bothered me. It was the isolation after a meal that I found depressing, so over the years, we developed a routine where I would shut down the kitchen while Lee drank his after-dinner coffee and kept me company.

Sipping his coffee, Lee takes in the kitchen and sighs. "We didn't have to do much to this space to make it work for you, just update the electrical and lighting, and clear the ventilation shaft for the oven." Glancing at the La Cornue, he shakes his head. "You're right, it is a jewel. And I know how much you love to use it, especially with the new recipes you've been developing. Back in Virginia, I was busy juggling projects and never realized how much time you put into your creations. I'm sorry I let my demons get the better of me this morning."

"Thanks for noticing how much time I spend cooking for you." I whip my dishtowel at him, lightly smacking his forearm with the corner. "Come spring, I'll be spending more time in the garden again, and Wendy will be the chef de maison. Until then, perhaps we can plan a trip to Paris, visit a few museums, dine at La Tour d'Argent, and stop by La Cornue to see if anyone can tell us more about Monsieur and why he received one of the first Le Château models. I checked the serial number, it's number 5. From everything I've read, there's been a waiting list for these things since before they were built."

"I only have a few small projects to get the house ready for Dave and Wendy's family in March. They should be done in plenty of time for their spring break visit. Hey, how about you and I go to Paris while the family's here?"

"It's a date!" I exclaim.

Lee grins self-satisfied with his grand apology.

Sensing the right time for a bit of ribbing, I grin. "Now, about those spotlights for my baby. Do you think this white light is good, or do you think a cooler blue bulb would highlight her better?" I wink and jump back as Lee swats at me. We laugh together, remembering why we fell in love in the first place.

10

A Little Bird Told Me

GREG, MARCH 2012

MY ARMS STRAIN AS THE SCREE UNDER MY FEET GIVES WAY, AND I pull my body over the ridge. One more heave and I'm standing at the edge of a rocky outcrop overlooking fields of grapes. Gashes on the slopes look as though a giant dragon has swooped out of the sky to snatch at prey, leaving behind furrows of rocky soil. The clearings pepper the hillsides at inclines so steep that it seems only sure-footed mountain goats could access them. I imagine satyrs of myth, baskets across their backs, harvesting the grapes.

Stepping back from the edge, I survey the path of my ascent. The climb turned out to be more strenuous than I had planned. My ropes would have made things easier, but Mom said, "No disappearing into the mountains for days at a time" and forbade me from packing my equipment. She was right. Had I brought my equipment, I'd have been tempted to spend most of my time here in the Dentelles de Montmirail.

But then again, I'm not sure the weather would have allowed it. Most of this week has been bitterly cold with the Mistral blowing down the Rhône Valley. Inside the protective walls of the villa, it's been cold enough. I can only imagine what it would have been like to be exposed to the wind on the side of a mountain. Besides, I don't relish being batted around like a toy at the end of a string.

Luckily, our last day of vacation had been forecast to be sunny and calm. Uncle Dave suggested I wait till the sun rose to leave the villa.

It was good advice. The departmental roads here aren't very wide but get off them and you're faced with roads so narrow that cars take turns crossing bridges. Only after I turned off the engine, the car snuggled in the brush at the side of the road, did I release my death grip on the steering wheel and take a deep breath. I thought "If my climb is as challenging as the drive to get here, I'm in for a great day."

I began the climb shivering and wondering if the exertions of my muscles would be able to keep up with the heat I was losing to the rock before me. But my timing was perfect. Pulling myself above the trees at the base of the cliff, the first rays of the sun began to peak through the cleft of the hills behind me. As I advanced, the sun rose, and the rock before me began to warm.

How I love the strain of my muscles, the balance in my body as my weight shifts from the pull of my fingertips to the push of my toes. Climbing demands my presence. I focus on the here and now, just me and the rock. There is no space for anything else in my mind. This is peace.

Tomorrow, we fly back to the States, and this respite ends. Back to work, back to an empty apartment, back to the malaise of my life. I shake my head to clear my mind and focus on the landscape. The climb has evoked emotions that cause a feeling of déjà vu.

I am taken back to the summer between my junior and senior years in college, sitting on the edge of the Grand Canyon after our last rafting tour of the season. I was feeling happy and fulfilled and didn't want to leave. But my logical self was a worm working through my brain, telling me not to waste the three years I'd already put into my degree. The summer had been a dream, crewing for the tour company on the Colorado. I had felt the adrenaline ignite my senses with each rapid and a pleasant exhaustion as I fell to sleep under the starry sky.

And yet my mind whispered, "What about the money your parents have shelled out for you? Are you really going to disappoint them?"

It was as though my body and my mind were at war. My mind won, and I went back to school. From there, it was down the rabbit hole.

I didn't have plans for after graduation, so I wandered through the job fair on campus and received an offer as an area manager for Virginia Management, an East Coast logistics company, and started earning money.

I was good at what I did—organizing things and people. I'm a good leader, so the company paid for leadership training, and I climbed the corporate ladder. Last year, they made me manager of a new office— new title, bigger paycheck, and less satisfaction with life.

That's when I started climbing every weekend and every vacation. I needed to clear my head. It was the stress of the new job, I told myself. Using my body made me feel alive again. That didn't go over well with Laura, the woman everyone thought I'd marry, including me. The last straw was the week-long climb in the Davis Mountains over Thanksgiving. By Christmas, it was obvious our future together was rocky, and by New Year's, "we" were a thing of the past.

I guess it's a good thing Aunt Wendy and Uncle Dave had to re-schedule our visit from Christmas to spring break. Laura and I wouldn't have been good company at Christmas.

I began the new year with Laura's words ringing in my ears, "You have no ambition. No goals! All you do is run away. I can't live like that. I need a partner who wants to build a future." I was determined to prove her wrong. I threw myself into my work. I took on new projects and pushed to improve our numbers. With no one to go home to, I spent long hours at my desk. But in the end, I felt no better. The mountains called to me.

Laura had been right. I didn't see myself making money for Virginia Management in the future. I had been running away. But what do I want to do with my future? I do this job well. I make good money. Isn't that the American dream? Someone once said, "Just because you can, doesn't mean you should." How true.

A breeze brings me back to Provence and the peak on which I stand. I shiver and realize I need to keep moving. After taking in the views from the ridge and scouting new routes for future climbs, I make my way back to the foot of the cliff and Uncle Dave's car.

Of everyone in the family, Uncle Dave's the one who gets me. I'm glad I could help him choose bikes for the guests. I think he was a bit overwhelmed, though, when I got technical with the guy at the bike shop, discussing cycling the hills in Provence, especially when we delved into my dream of riding to the top of Mt. Ventoux. Uncle Dave had to bring us back to the mission at hand, purchasing bikes for "regular" people. We settled on a few bikes that were sturdy enough for the surrounding hills, but nothing too technical. Uncle Dave said, "People just want to wander the French countryside in search of a photo op to show their friends when they get home."

Before our trip, Mom insisted we all read something "appropriate." Being the child of educators has always meant homework before a trip. For Mom and Dad, appropriate reading included articles on the wineries of the Côtes du Rhône. Megan read a bunch of romance novels set in Provence. Really? How did she get away with that? Me, I chose history. I always choose history. My connection to history makes Dad laugh and ask Mom if maybe he missed something between her and his college roommate, Nate. Nate went on to get a PhD in history while Dad went the English route. Mom ruffles my blond hair and smiles—it was Dad's curly blond hair that first attracted her to him.

My reading began with an overview of the area's past - the Romans. Those guys were all over the northern Med. In fact, Provence was once a province of the Roman Empire. To the Romans, it was just "the province." The overview went on to say, "Signs of this early Roman expansion can still be seen in the amphitheaters, arenas, and aqueducts that remain to this day." They sure knew how to build things in the first century. It's hard to believe anything built today will be around in another hundred years, much less two thousand.

I buzzed through the centuries until I got to the stuff about World War II and the Vichy Government. You know, in the movies and news reels I've seen the French people welcomed the Allied troops, showering them with gratitude. I always thought they had been unwillingly occupied, but what I read about the Vichy government made me question all of that.

In 1939, the French and the British declared war on Germany for invading Poland. Everyone was prepared for a war that wasn't turning out to be a war. Each army sat on its own side of the Maginot Line for months. After a while, everyone took to calling it the Phony War. Then the Germans blitzkrieged through the Netherlands and Belgium, around the Maginot Line. Basically, the Germans bit the French in the butt and put the French government in a tailspin.

The French Third Republic fell apart. The National Assembly dissolved itself and gave General Pétain, a revered World War I hero, absolute power. Pétain signed an armistice with Nazi Germany, and France became a collaborator in the German drive to rule the world. It all happened so fast! The French weren't crazy about it, but the agreement meant their sons and husbands would come home, and the countryside would be spared the plague of another war, the last one still too fresh in their memories.

The deposed Prime Minister and his cabinet had other ideas, though. The Prime Minister sent his Undersecretary of War, De Gaulle, to London to get Churchill's support and headed to Morocco with a few generals to make plans. Turns out De Gaulle was the only one to make it out of the country.

So, it was Pétain's Vichy government that ran France during the war. And it was the Vichy government that worked with the Nazis to round up Jews and enforce Nazi laws. At the same time, De Gaulle was in London calling for France to resist the Nazis. What a confusing time to be French. They were being ruled by a government that had thrown in with the invaders while their former Undersecretary for War was encouraging them to remember their beliefs in liberté, égalité, fraternité, and to resist. So many questions filled my mind.

There's Roman history all over Provence, but what happened in the 1940s is nowhere to be seen. I have spent the past week looking for clues to what happened. The French are proud of their Roman ruins and the history they mark, but I didn't see anything about what happened in World War II.

My history search may not have gone well, but I was able to get out on a few sunny afternoons when the winds died down. I checked out a couple of biking destinations close to the villa. The Caderousse Locks aren't too far, and the path includes a stretch where the plane trees canopy the road, making the outing a "twofer"—a short ride AND that quintessential photo op. Watching the boats make their way up and down the river was fascinating, and I'd have loved to stay longer, but the wind kicked up, convincing me it was time to return to the protection of the villa's walls.

Another day, I decided to take a spin to Châteauneuf-du-Pape, something for the wine lovers who were sure to visit. I tried to convince Mom and Dad to join me. They just mumbled something about riding back to the villa into the wind, screwing up a good buzz. Hopefully, they'll give it a try when they return this summer.

I think the best outing, though, was to the fortress overlooking Mornas, an ancient citadel that sits high above the valley floor. The Count of Toulouse chose wisely when he built the fortress there in the 12th century. From the walls, they could see what was happening up and down the river and protect the town below. Being a climber and not a Count, though, I found the view over my shoulder more interesting. Mount Ventoux rose in the distance, and the Dentelles broke the horizon with their jagged peaks. My heart fluttered at the thought of future climbs and a challenging bike ride. Ah! Mount Ventoux, I will return for you. My brush with medieval history taught me one thing - I am happy to be alive today, no privies or huddling in front of smoky fireplaces for me.

Uncle Dave seemed pleased with the maps and brief tour descriptions that I left for the guests. I offered to bring my mountain bike next time and work up a trip to Mt. Ventoux and back, but he assured me that any guests wanting to make that trip would come prepared.

Having made quick work of rappelling down the cliff, I make my way back to the car and take a last longing look before dropping into the driver's seat. Before taking off my boots, I lean back to take a long draw from my water bottle. As I'm straightening up, my eye catches the movement of a small bird. I get the feeling he's watching me. He cocks his head from side to side as if trying to get a better look. Moving nearer the end of the branch, he looks down at me. Once again, he tilts his head, and I hear, "Where are you going?"

"Back to the villa," I respond aloud.

The bird turns his head to the other side. "And then?"

"Home, I guess." Something at the back of my mind is tugging at me.

The bird hops back and forth along the branch and finally settles back at my end. "Are you sure?"

Now I'm beginning to doubt my sanity. Having a conversation with a bird is weird enough, but its question is like a seed rapidly taking over my brain.

"Where's home?"

"Richmond." I lean forward, resting my elbows on my knees. "But if Richmond is home, why am I always running away?" I think aloud. Now I'm hacked. I'm talking to a bird looking for answers to a question I'd rather not think about, much less hear from a bird. "I was having a great day until you showed up," I sneer.

"Me? Or the thought of going home?"

"You wouldn't understand." I look up. "It's complicated."

The bird inclines his head as though considering my plight. Finally, he puffs up his feathers, shakes himself out, and settles on the branch. "I've got time."

"I've got a job. I've got responsibilities. It must be nice being a bird. Not worrying about getting things right."

"Getting what right?"

"Life! Getting life right. How do you know when you've got it right?"

"You're happy."

"Well, I'm definitely NOT that."

"Why not?"

"Good question. According to the numbers, I should be happy. I make big bucks, have a great condo, and drive a nice car." I shake my head slowly as the other side of the story tumbles from my lips. "I did have a woman who wanted to spend her life with me. But I ran her off. I hate my job, and my mom gives me those sad eyes when she catches me staring into space." I rub my head, willing the pain to stop. "All I want is some peace."

"It's pretty peaceful right here." The bird looks about.

"Yeah, tell me about it. The view today was perfect. I felt like I could see tomorrow."

"What does that look like?"

"Tomorrow? A cage."

"Oh, now THAT I understand. No one likes being in a cage."

"Yeah, and I built this one myself."

"Then open the door!"

"I wish." I shake my head and feel a tightness in my chest.

"It's your cage. You choose. In or out?"

"What would that even look like?"

"More days like today."

"Yeah, this has been one spectacular day, even if I did end up talking to a bird." There's a crunching sound off to my right. My eyes follow a small tractor as it bounces by on the road. As it nears, I pull the door in close and exchange nods with the driver. When the tractor rounds the bend in the road, I push the door wide and look up at the branch. No bird. I stand and walk around the tree, checking out every branch. "Hey," Where'd you go? You can't leave in the middle of the conversation. You haven't told me the answer yet."

What the hell? I have lost my mind! I am in the middle of France, looking for a little brown bird to give me the answer to life. I stomp back to the car, climb in, and slam the door. Shoving my hand in my pocket, I struggle to find the key, too stubborn to open the door and stand up. My frustration boils over, and I find myself hanging on to the steering wheel as though I will disappear if I let it go.

My anger finally subsides. Breathing raggedly, I feel the answer slowly fill my body, and I relax. I deserve to be happy, and I am happiest when I'm climbing, riding, or hiking—moving my body through nature. THIS is my happy place.

Sitting up straight, I shake my head and breathe deeply. I reach for my pocket and find the keys hanging out. I laugh to myself. When the student is ready … I smile, put the car in reverse, and back out of the brush. I know which direction I am going from here, and I'm ready to make plans to get myself there. There's got to be a nature travel company out there looking for a good logician, and if there's not, I'll start my own.

Returning to the villa, I slow for the dip after taking time to read the sign on the gate, printed in both French and English.

Leave the World Behind, Enjoy Life.

That's just what I did this week, and what I plan to do from now on. I don't have to worry about the rest of the world, just me, and I'm going to be happy doing it. Thank you, Uncle Dave and Aunt Wendy, for finding your happy place; it turned out to be the place that I found myself.

11

The Voice in My Head

CLAIRE, MAY 2012

JUST BEFORE SUNRISE, THE BIRDS BEGIN THEIR SYMPHONY, THE strength of the ensemble increasing until the crescendo when the sun's rays reach around the edge of the earth to reassure its avian alarm clock that yes, the call for a new day has been heard. As the sun's rays slowly illuminate the room, I know that going back to sleep is out of the question.

Careful to avoid the squeaky floorboards, I carefully slip out of the seemingly deserted house, feeling a whoosh of air as the massive door closes behind me. A slight shiver runs through my body, but I know it will disappear once I get moving. Gravel crunching under my feet punctuates the morning anthem that engulfs me. At the gate, a quick kick and my morning jog has begun. Soon, my heart is pumping rhythmically, and I join the day.

I find myself running along the river, watching the flotsam of life from upstream make its way to Avignon and beyond. The vines in the field to my right are filled with small green grapes waiting for the sun to warm them. Having grown up in a fly-over state where topsoil is a foot thick, I have no idea how anything can grow in this dry, rocky soil.

Surrounded by this beauty, I yearn to release the tightness in my chest and the churning of my stomach. What's wrong with me? I've dreamed of the south of France since I read Peter Mayle's Year in Provence. Even the romancey Under the Tuscan Sun didn't shake my yearning to walk among the lavender and watch the sunflowers shift with the passing of the day. Reading Ms. Lowrey's collection of French travel guides, romance novels, and murder mysteries while I babysat her daughter carried me away. They helped me forget about small-town life and its mundane worries. Those dreams are what brought me here. They are what made me study, earn a scholarship, and believe in a life beyond the cornfields of Kansas.

I'm here! In Provence. I'm running next to the Rhône River watching the sun rise above the grapes, and this damn Gordian knot won't unravel. How can I enjoy myself while the voice in my head whispers, "Who do you think you are? A trip to Provence, really?"

I thought a run would help. After all these years, you'd think I'd be able to shake off the old Midwestern work ethic: "Work hard and be happy with a vacation visiting relatives in the next state." I can afford this trip. I own my condo. I have money in the bank, and I DO work hard. Is it so bad to have a dream that takes me beyond Kansas? This is my dream, damn it. I've earned it and I'm going to enjoy it. Tears stream down my cheeks. How many times have I had this argument with myself? When will the old tapes wear out and quit tugging at my subconscious?

I love Lilly and Beth, but they wouldn't understand. Life for them has always been easy. Their stories of high school spring breaks of being snow bunnies on the mountainsides of Vale are so distant from my spring breaks, taking care of my brothers, and reading about adventure. And their fairy-tale lives continue. They both have husbands who think nothing of them celebrating their ten-year college reunion together, in a mansion, in Provence. And as part of the package, the guys splurged on first-class tickets to get them here!

A husband I could depend on would be lovely. After years of living with Joey's ever-changing dreams, I was looking for an exit, not a ring. Has it been a year already since I told him I was done with his impulsive lifestyle and unpredictable income? When we met, his edginess was sexy. I never knew what to expect: the opening of a trendy restaurant, a stay in the penthouse suite of a high-rise hotel, or a last-minute getaway to a romantic B&B. He swept me away with the excitement, but that damned voice kept whispering to me, "This isn't your kind of life." I guess the voice was right. That didn't work out.

Lilly and Beth didn't understand my relief when it was over. They'd spent their entire lives basking in the sun at the deep end of the pool while I paddled in the shallows where I could always touch bottom. Oh well, Joey's gone. I'm safe. And lonely. And numb. This trip was supposed to change that. So far, it hasn't worked.

Last night, the girls sat on the patio into the wee hours, allowing their midwestern bio-clocks to adjust to French time. They slept on the trans-Atlantic flight, lying flat in their first-class seats, arriving refreshed and ready for their day. I, who refused to waste money on such frivolities, purchased a tourist seat and spent ten and a half hours from Dallas to Paris contorted in a space my Schnauzer wouldn't have been able to wind himself into. The lack of sleep from the trip only added to my frazzled state after anxious weeks of preparation. Maybe it had been the lack of sleep, or maybe I didn't want to endure the chirpy conversation the girls were having. Whatever, I was happy to be in bed early, even before the sun was fully set.

As much as I love Lilly and Beth, I've always felt like an outsider. Not that they haven't tried to make me feel at home in their world. They were the ones who got me through homecoming our first year. An SMU gala is nothing like the dances I attended in a sweaty midwestern gym strategically lit to create the small-town version of intimacy. Somehow, I let them help me pay for a dress from the sale section of one of those fancy-dress shops in Preston Center. Lilly even set me up with a date—a sad guy from her biology class whose girlfriend had dumped him the week before.

For a girl from the plains of Kansas, growing up surrounded by corn, life in Dallas, Highland Park to be specific, was like taking a carnival goldfish from its tiny bowl and throwing it into the ocean filled with exotic fish. I had known I wanted out of Kansas, and to attend a good business school—I needed to be rich to make my way to France. So, I enlisted my high school counselor to help me apply to universities that met that criteria. Years of reading and the drive to get out of the state landed me three full scholarships, one on each coast and one in Dallas, a straight shot south on I-35. Of course, my parents thought Dallas would be best, so there I was.

When Beth plopped into the seat next to me in Economics 1311, I had no idea how my life would change. I helped her with numbers, and she helped me with life in Big D. Once we met Lilly, we became the female Three Musketeers, a theme I had to explain to my rich, well-traveled friends, whose literary experience was remarkably lacking. Somehow, my book knowledge and their real-life experience fit together. By the time we graduated, we had built a strong bond of friendship behind which I did my best to keep the voice of doubt.

Listening to the new day begin this morning was lovely, though. The birdsong floated in, and I could hear the church bells in the distance. The room was cool, and I was tempted to snuggle deeper into the covers. I'm glad Wendy suggested I leave the windows open. What a great morning for a run. The cool, dry air is so different from yesterday's scorching sun that greeted us when we stepped from the train in Avignon. Thankfully, the thick stone walls of the villa and the shade of the trees create an oasis. Something about the place says, "Relax, you're safe." Maybe that's why I slept so well. I hardly noticed the girls' conversation or laughter from the patio.

My cool down takes me past rows of melons in a field near the villa. Halfway across the field, an old man uses a pole to poke at hidden fruit among the leaves. Suddenly, a barking dog bounds over to meet me, his wagging tail propelling him over the mounds of fruit.

"Hi, little guy! How are you on this beautiful morning?"

Bending, I scratch this friendly pup behind the ears and am rewarded with a quick swipe of his tongue across my cheek.

"Chien!" The old man calls.

I stand and wave at the man who waves back as if shooing away a fly.

"Chien!" He calls again.

"Looks like your daddy's calling." One last scratch to the back of Chien's head, and he bounds back across the field. I stood for a while taking in the day. The duo moves along the row, with the old man pointing out melons and the dog sniffing.

I've read about dogs trained to ferret out truffles, but I've never heard of a melon sniffing dog. After watching for a few minutes, I figured out that melons receiving a wag of the tail and a glance at the master are rolled into the path between the rows. I can only guess that someone a bit younger and more agile will be retrieving the Chien-approved fruits.

Passing through the gates of the villa, I realize that the tension in my body has eased. I pause to read the sign.

Laissez le monde derrière vous, ralentissez et profitez de la vie.

Leave the world behind, enjoy life.

I am willing to leave the world behind. It may still be there when I leave in six days, but this week I am determined to enjoy life.

MEOW! There's the cat! What's her name? Oh yeah, Le Chat—the cat. Sounds so exotic in French. Whoops, there goes her tail around the side of the house. I wonder what she's up to. I walk between the house and the wall where lush vines grow. More grapes. They're everywhere! I wonder if they also make wine from these grapes.

Surveying the neatly laid-out garden, I spy Le Chat wandering among the herbs. There goes that tail again. My leg brushes the plants as I pass, and the scent of rosemary enchants me. Le Chat's path has led to the back of the garden, where I find myself in the arms of an ancient tree.

This is one gnarly tree, and those are figs! They look luscious. Why not? I reach out and gently pull a fig from its branch. The ripe fruit collapses in my hand, and its juice runs down my forearm. I've never tasted a fig like this before. Mm, soft, sweet, and oh so sticky. I think I'll have another. This has got to be what heaven is like.

Licking my fingers, I notice the fountain. Washing the evidence of my sins from my hands, I surreptitiously glance over my shoulder. Surely, I'm not the first person to think of this. Perched on the edge of the fountain, I absorb the world around me. I am in Eden. Who would want to live anywhere else? I relax and take it all in the warmth of the sun, the music of the fountain, and the purr of Le Chat rubbing against my leg. My shoulders relax even more as they slide down my back, and I realize I am breathing deeply, taking in the scent of the herbs. I could get used to this.

I finally decide that I am ready to join the rest of the world. Au revoir, Le Chat. Thanks for the tour. The scent of fresh-baked croissants envelops me as I step through the kitchen door to find Wendy arranging the pastries on a plate. Beside her on the counter is a spread of cheese and fruit to accompany the flaky delicacies.

Wendy cheerfully greets me. "Good morning! You were out early."

"Well, I did go to bed rather early."

"It's pretty normal for guests to make their own bedtimes, especially after a long trip."

"I followed Le Chat on a tour of the yard. The scent of rosemary hypnotized me, and I couldn't help but follow her." Reflecting on the experience, I feel a sense of satisfaction.

"This has been her domain for years. She's been generous enough to allow us to share it with her."

Taking a fig from a bowl, I hold it to the light and examine its perfection. "I had a few of these fresh from the tree, but I think I can squeeze in one more".

Wendy laughs. "It's days like these that we feel like we're living in our own Garden of Eden."

"That's what I called it! I was sitting on the side of the fountain, mesmerized by the morning. I felt as though I'd stumbled into Eve's domain."

The two of us sit in silence, sharing a personal moment of gratitude.

"Nice breakfast spread!"

"It's what we put out for American guests. Breakfast for the French is a little more than an espresso and a chunk of baguette or pastry."

"Well, I'm ready to try out your American French breakfast."

The girls are still asleep, and the rest of the residents are off for the day, so I sit at the counter keeping Wendy company as she prepares vegetables for lunch. After smashing a few garlic cloves, she chops zucchini and eggplant, which I learn to call courgette and aubergine. A generous splash of olive oil, a sprinkle of salt, and the sheets of vegetables go into the oven. Wendy sets the timer and makes a cup of coffee for herself.

"So, tell me about your plans for the week. Lilly was going on and on last night about visiting the Palais des Papes, and Beth is excited for the wine tasting and cooking class in Châteauneuf-du-Pape. What are you looking forward to?"

"My dream has always been to BE in France. To experience France, not run around seeing how many tourist sights I can tag before time's up. I want to know what it feels like to be French. This morning was a great start. The special feeling of the air, the sun rising over the grapes, the waters of the Rhône flowing toward the sea. This is what I have been looking forward to." I pass my arm in front of me, taking in her breakfast and the kitchen.

"So wise, and at such a young age. I had to stumble through the gates of paradise before I learned that lesson."

"When I was a kid, I used to watch Rick Steves on PBS. He spoke about travel as an experience, one that allows you to get to know a country and its people. He'd share a meal with the people he met and listen to their stories, and they'd laugh together. I need to laugh."

Wendy chuckles. "I'm not sure we laugh with the French or if they are just laughing at us, but we do enjoy the few locals who have chosen to befriend us."

"When Lilly and Beth said they wanted to come to Provence and stay in a villa, I was relieved. I was afraid they were going to choose Paris. Don't get me wrong, one day I will see Paris, but for my first taste of La République, this is perfect. "

Wendy reaches out and squeezes my hand in understanding. "I think we can help you with your French experience. Thursday is market day in Orange. The market is an adventure. It's been around since the 15th century and is open for business every Thursday, rain or shine. Of course, the food changes with the seasons, but you never know what else you'll find. Besides the food, there are all kinds of clothes and jewelry, a local vendor selling handmade linens, exquisite perfumes, and a wide range of art. There's no rhyme or reason to the way things are laid out either. Last week, Dave and I stood side by side. He bought cheese while I debated on which bracelet looked best with my outfit. That disjointedness drives him crazy, but he wouldn't miss a market day for anything."

"Yes! The market is exactly what I want to do. Let's see, I've told the girls I'll go to Avignon with them on Monday for a tour of the Palais des Papes and then have lunch at some restaurant Lilly found on Yelp. On Tuesday, we will visit the arena and cathedrals in Nîmes. On Wednesday, they haven't decided if they want to go to Sète for a day on the coast or wander around the port area of Marseille. I prefer Sète. When I go home, I want to be able to tell people I swam in the Mediterranean. Thursday, there's a wine tasting and cooking classes with a chef, and Friday, they want to do a day of shopping in Aix-en-Provence."

"That's quite an itinerary."

"I've only agreed to Avignon, Nîmes, and Sète, if that's where they decide to go. The rest I'll decide on later."

"Today's Sunday, so the only places open in L'Esprit du Rhône are the café and the patisserie. That's why I'm roasting veggies. Today, your provincial adventure begins with a cold roast vegetable salad, accompanied by cheese, sausage, bread, and, of course, wine. Newly arrived visitors, especially those who arrive on Saturday, usually sleep in, eat a late breakfast, and only want an early evening meal. Sundays in France are a time for family. Unless you're in a tourist area, there's not much to do but relax and plan your week."

Wendy walks to the desk and pulls a few pamphlets from the display. "Here are some places to consider. They're close enough that you can get to them on one of our bikes. If you're a rider, you can choose the ones further away; they usually end up being an all-day affair unless you're my nephew, who always seems to be in training for one race or another. Then it's just a quick sprint up the road, Aunt Wendy." Wendy imitates her nephew. "I'd offer to make you a picnic lunch, but it's more French to drop into a local café and order the plat du jour. I'll give you a water bottle to hook onto the bike. The rest of your trip is an adventure to be written as the day unfolds."

"Thanks, I'll check them out." I scoop up the pamphlets and head for my room. As I pass through the solarium, the view of the garden catches my attention.

"What is it about the light in Provence? It stops me in my tracks and makes me see things in a different light. I feel like I'm walking through a painting."

Wendy smiles, "I know what you mean. To me, Cézanne's and Matisse's paintings are like travel posters for the soul. They call to us, saying Come, drink in the countryside and enjoy life. I'm pretty sure the Monsieur understood that when he hung that sign on the front gate all those years ago."

Nodding dreamily, I wander away.

The tour of the Palais des Papes was fascinating, though its history is just another example of how the battle for power divided a religion built on a message of love. In my mind, the money spent on the grandeur of the church and the few who lived within its walls sharply contrasts with the struggles of the faithful who lived outside. Not for the first time in my life do I find the history of a religion I was raised to honor to be not only disappointing but downright embarrassing. Shaking off my disillusionment, I open my eyes to the beauty around me. I've been wandering the streets of Avignon since the girls and I parted ways after lunch.

I must admit that Lilly was right about the restaurant she'd chosen for lunch. We walked past it twice before realizing it was the place that housed the modern chef who created old-fashioned French cuisine. There was a reason Lilly had needed to make reservations weeks before. The place was tiny, three tables in the front and six at the back. Lilly had requested the garden view. I think she was disappointed with the small herb garden nestled within the wall of the surrounding buildings. But I was mesmerized by the beauty of the symmetrical paths and the perfectly arranged collection of herbs and greens. Lilly's disappointment didn't last long, though. She perked up when the bottle of crisp rosé arrived. There was no order to be placed. Everyone received the plat du jour, within their personal dietary needs. Since all three of us are omnivores with no restrictions, we were treated to what was described as "le dîner du Dimanche de grand-mère." If only my grandmother had prepared something this delicious for Sunday dinner.

The meal was as beautiful as it was delicious. I gazed at the first course, soupe d'asperges, not wanting to disturb the swirls of cream with perfectly designed croutons that composed the miniature work of art. But once I tasted it, I was glad I had. The main course, poulet rôti au fenouil et riz à l'oignon and not listed, but always plated with a French meal, une petite salade verte. I had never had chicken and rice like this before. What was their secret? When I return to Dallas, I'm going to have to open that Julia Child cookbook my mother bought me as a housewarming gift. A small plate of cheeses followed the plat du jour, each one chosen to accompany the warm fennel taste left in our mouths from the meal. Just when we thought it couldn't get any better, a mouthwatering slice of lemon tart was set before us. Each bite of the small confection hit the tongue with a creamy sweetness that melted into the tangy taste of lemon and ended with the crunchy sugariness of the crust. The textures and flavors playing on the tongue left us begging for more. Alas, after finishing the last bite, the best we could ask for was the bitterness of an exquisite espresso.

Yes, lunch had been the French experience I had dreamed of. But now I need a walk. The girls are excited to shop at the boutiques for fashions no one at home will be wearing, but I am in search of something else I won't find at home - a French neighborhood.

I ramble down one cobblestone street after another, stepping over high curbs and down into small alleyways, taking time to appreciate the various balconies and admiring the centuries-old wrought ironwork. The city is quiet with people finishing their lunch hour. Once in a while, I catch the sound of plates being cleared from a dinner table, or laughter and conversation of diners not ready to return to work.

Lost in thought, I run my hand along a wrought iron fence and nearly collide with a woman unlocking a gate. "Sorry!"

"No problem. Would you like to visit our collection?"

"Yes, please." I read the sign, Musée Calvet. "What kind of collection is it?"

"A bit of everything, the usual sculptures and paintings, some Egyptian antiquities, a few prehistoric finds, and a bit of Islamic Art. All housed in this jewel box of a mansion."

"Now I have to come in!" Together we walk towards the entrance of the ticket office. "You sound American."

"That's because I am." She extends her hand, "I'm Jennifer."

I shake her hand. "I'm Claire. So, how does an American girl find her way to a life in Avignon?"

"I landed a prized spot as a summer international guide at the Palais a few years back. I was loving the job and life here in Avignon, trying to figure out how to stay when the summer was over. I'm not sure if it's my curiosity or my background in art history, but I found myself badgering the art director almost daily with questions about the paintings in the halls. When the PR director needed help at one of the city's cultural events—a soirée for the wealthy to donate to the arts—the director suggested I assist. I think he just wanted to keep me busy and out of his way. Anyway, that's where I met Michel, the director here." Jennifer inclines her head towards the building. "He was working with the Art Institute of Chicago, arranging a traveling exhibit. The process came with numerous documents, all of which were in English. I offered to help. When my time at the Palais was up, we were in the middle of processing the exhibit, so Michel hired me." Laughing to herself, "Turns out that asking lots of questions does pay off. Now I live in the heart of Provence, where I enjoy great food, work with museums worldwide, and appreciate life. And you?" Jennifer looks around. "You a lone traveler?"

"No, I came with two college friends. We're celebrating our ten-year college graduation. We decided we'd rather come to France than pay for a weekend in the city we already work in." Jennifer nods in understanding. "They're shopping. I'm taking in the streets of Avignon."

"And your walk brought you here! Take a look at our jewel box and let me know what you think. I like to say that our collection is large enough to touch the soul without being so big that it overwhelms the senses."

"Thanks, I will."

Beyond an art appreciation class I took as an elective my sophomore year, I don't know a lot about art, but Jennifer's joy makes me want to learn more. Jennifer's description had been perfect. The hall of sculptures fills me with awe. I stare thoughtfully into the eyes of the wise sage whose visage looks out over the ages. Contemplating the toes of the young hunter sheathed in sandals of rope makes me want to reach out to dust the dirt from his feet. How do they do it? How do sculptors turn blocks of marble into figures you expect to step from their pedestals?

When I've seen enough finely turned muscles of marble, I find myself in a series of rooms displaying paintings, one filled with landscapes of the area, one that displays historic scenes, and then two filled with portraits. But my favorite paintings are those of myths and magic. In this gallery, my imagination runs wild, and I think about how much there is that I never dreamt of. As I tire of paintings, I discover a gallery filled with Egyptian art. Here I am standing before a brightly adorned sarcophagus. I wonder if the mummy who planned on a trip to The Field of Reeds is lurking the halls of the museum, wondering what kind of afterlife she's ended up in.

I glance at my watch and think that the girls are probably on their second gin and tonics as they wait for me in the square. I'd better get going. I'm sorry, I don't have time to find Jennifer and thank her for her recommendation.

Humming to myself, I weave between people on the street. Bounding around a sharp corner, I come face to face with a woman who looks familiar. I take a second look and realize it's my reflection. I look into the woman's eyes and discover she is someone I've never seen before.

This woman is happy and satisfied with life. The difference between who I saw in the mirror this morning and this reflection is magical. Whatever spell the museum cast on me, I am happy to be charmed by it.

The plaza is filled with people, and I find the girls as expected, sitting at a café in the shade of a plane tree, with gin & tonic glasses before them. Their faces are a mixture of anger and relief.

"We were worried we'd lost our Third Musketeer!" blurts out Lilly.

"What would a trip to France be without the three of us getting into trouble together?" Beth chimes in.

My heart warms as I realize how much these women mean to me. The world around me seems to freeze as I take it in: the table where my friends sit, empty glasses before them, the breeze that crosses my shoulders, and the voices of the milling crowd droning in the plaza. The flapping of the banners on the top of the Palais catches my eye, and I think, this is what I have dreamed of. Being here, experiencing this. Looking back at my friends' relieved faces, I realize that I am the reason the Three Musketeers have come to Provence. My friends have done this for me! The spell breaks, and I laugh. "All for one, and one for all!"

The week has been filled with history, sun, and sand, as well as good food and great wine. Since that afternoon in Avignon, I have enjoyed the adventure. The best part has been being a Musketeer again and remembering why the three of us became friends.

I have been living my dream. On Tuesday, we tromped up and down the stairs of the Nîmes amphitheater in search of a gladiator to liven up my nonexistent love life. On the beach in Sète, I gave in to the topless sunbathing culture. I laugh when I think of how my strapless suntan could have covered my entire body if we had followed Lilly's directions to the nude beach further down the peninsula. While I lay topless on the Mediterranean sands, I watched the toddlers play naked in the surf as roving bands of topless grandmas savored the sun and their time together. The thin, the fat, the young, the old, everyone was enjoying themselves, exposing more skin than I see in the locker room at the Y. Europeans are so much freer. They are free to be happy. Yes, that is the gift this week has given me, the freedom to be satisfied.

It's Friday, and the girls have gone to Aix-en-Provence for one last day of shopping. Shopping isn't the way I want to spend my last day in France. I want time to appreciate my dream come true and say goodbye to France my way.

Water bottle in hand, I hop on the bike Dave left for me at the front door and head into the French countryside. I take in the ubiquitous fields of grapes interspersed with fields of melons, lavender, and sunflowers. The drying soil begins to bake as the sun rises higher. My path takes me across streams and ditches filled with water from last night's rain. From the map, I can tell my route is running close to the Rhône. I'm glad Wendy's nephew highlighted this map. One wrong turn and I'd find myself in the river.

I hear the crunch of the gravel under the bike's tires as I glide along, taking in the countryside. I love the country homes of Provence. How is it that the French can make a sand-colored box look so inviting? The style hasn't changed much since the Romans closed in the walls with terracotta tiles, and someone painted the shutters blue. Windows underscored with boxes of brightly colored flowers, paths of gravel neatly outline beds of lavender, and gnarly old fig and olive trees add to the house's charm. What is it about such simple touches that makes this dusty countryside so inviting?

I have been busy appreciating the simple elegance of the house and don't notice the dog until he is barking at me and running along the edge of his field on the other side of a ditch. "Hi, buddy! Glorious day, isn't it?" I throw my head back and laugh as we move along together until the line of trees marking his territory calls him to a halt.

Oh, France, you have been everything I have ever dreamed of. For so long, you were that elusive hope that kept me moving forward. I should have met you years ago, but I never believed I could have my dream. Thank you, Beth & Lilly, for making it happen.

It's been a tiring ride, so I settle on a rock and let the view carry me away. Breathing deeply, I smell the rosemary and scrub plants growing on the hillside. I hear the breeze rustle the leaves and appreciate the warmth of the sun on my skin. The voice in the recesses of my mind struggles to get my attention, but I'm not listening to it anymore. I am here. I am living my dream, and it's going well. I'm ready to let go of this dream now. It did its job. It kept me moving forward, but now I'm ready for new dreams. What else do I want? Who do I want to be?

I close my eyes, and my mind wanders—visions of adventures I have never considered before float through my thoughts. The new possibilities fill me with happiness, the voice of the past no longer casting a shadow on my joy. I remember that my friends will be waiting for me back at the villa. Wendy is preparing a meal to pair with the wine we purchased in Châteauneuf-du-Pape earlier this week.

This week has been magical. Tonight, our final night, the Three Musketeers will fill the air of the villa's garden with laughter and stories of this adventure and new ones to come.

12

Crossroads

HARRIS & LIZ, JUNE 2012

HARRIS

I CAN'T BELIEVE SHE LEFT. TOMORROW IS OUR 25TH ANNIVERSARY, and she's left me alone at a villa in France because she "has to" return to Atlanta to save an account. I'm not sure if I feel worse that she's abandoned me in the middle of our vacation, or that she's letting life pass her by. How can Liz not think more of herself, of us? I don't care if she is a partner in the firm. The other partners can figure things out. She left everything in its usual form—organized and self-explanatory- so that everything they needed to complete the transaction was available without her. Why can't she just let things be?

Wiping the sweat from my face, I slow to a walk and look around. I have no idea how long I've been running. I'm not even sure where I am. The last thing I remember clearly is putting on my running shoes and going out the gate. My emotions were in turmoil, and I had to get away. I couldn't be there when she left.

Liz is on her way to Paris to catch a flight to Atlanta. When she told me she was leaving, I was in shock. I couldn't focus, and I was scared I'd say something I'd regret. There was just no way I was going to be the one to drive her to the train station in Avignon. That was asking too much.

Collapsing on a concrete abutment over a stream, I cradle my head in my hands. I am brokenhearted. Liz and the boys are everything to me. This trip was to be a celebration of all that we have accomplished. A time to dream of life as retirees, as people free from responsibilities. Not that we're ready to retire tomorrow, but why not begin daydreaming? Do some traveling? Get some ideas? Indulge in a few fantasies of what could be? Every time I broach the subject of retirement and my dream of living in France, Liz shuts me down with her laundry list of worries.

First, Jr. is getting married next spring. There's so much to be done between now and then.

Second, Kyle is all alone in California. He's so far away, trying to break into the movie business. How will he get by on his own? There must be something we can do to help him.

And third, the firm. There is so much more to do. How will it survive without me? I've put a lot of time and effort into building it! I can't walk away now. There's too much to do, and I'm not leaving it in the hands of the other partners.

From there, the conversation always devolves into Liz's lifelong obsession.

Atlanta has yet to hear of Elizabeth Shore! I will leave a legacy. The people of Atlanta will know Elizabeth Shore has been here. I will make a difference!

Not even last year's award as the best mid-sized law firm in Atlanta was enough. Liz still feels she must do more. When will it end? When will Liz understand her value and how much she is loved?

Ugh, I get to my feet and wander slowly back the way I came, hoping things will look familiar and that I will make the right turn at the crossroad.

Crossroads, I smile and laugh as I remember the day my path crossed Liz's for the first time. I was given the lead on developing several blocks in Midtown Atlanta after the MARTA (Metro Atlanta Rapid Transit Authority) opened a rail line there. The working name of the development was The Crossroads. I'd only been on the city staff for three years, and my boss had made me the lead planner. Of course, Larry kept an eye on things, but he trusted me to manage the paperwork and coordinate with the various city departments to complete the job. Ugh, the paperwork. That was the biggest nightmare, and where Liz became invaluable. She was interning for the law firm identified by the grant, and her boss had assigned the paperwork for the Midtown project to the new girl with a penchant for being well, anal. Her boss, Lloyd Linden, had been assigned the job, but Liz was so meticulous about dates and follow-through that he did little more than keep tabs on what Liz did. Of course, that didn't keep him from accepting a bonus from the firm for completing the job on time.

The first time we met, I couldn't make it to her office to review important papers because I had to be at The Crossroads with Leon Wright, an old-time contractor who had somehow managed to land a job the grant specified was open only to minority businesses. It turns out that women are a minority, and his wife was the official CEO of the company. He obviously knew how that game was played. He insisted that I meet him on-site to establish the date for the groundbreaking, which was more about the ceremony than getting any work done.

Since I couldn't go to her, she would bring the papers to me. As she said, "I have deadlines to meet."

"Aren't you a pretty little thing," began Wright. "You've got yourself a nice little secretary there, Harris."

Before I could correct him, Liz set the old man straight. "I am Elizabeth Shore. I am an intern at Howard, Angles & Linden, the legal office responsible for processing the paperwork you need to begin this project, and who you will continue to need if you expect to receive payment for your work. I am glad you find my looks pleasing, but it is my ability to process YOUR paperwork that should concern you most."

Caught between stunned embarrassment and anger, all Wright could muster was, "If you're going to be on a construction site, you'll need this." Glaring at her, he plopped a grossly oversized hard hat on her head. Liz gingerly balanced the hat on her 1980's "big hair," unloaded the forms for review onto the hood of his car and began to explain when each one needed to be returned to her at the law office so that they could be recorded with the appropriate authorities—city, state, and federal—and on exactly which dates that would be done. I wasn't sure which impressed me more, her comprehensive understanding and organization of the papers or her standing up to old man Wright, an icon in his own mind.

As the project progressed, I found myself more indebted to Liz's demanding ways. More than once, she saved my ass with a reminder of a deadline, no matter how seemingly minor.

Once the project was well underway, I thanked Liz for supporting the success of my first project. I made reservations at The Sun Dial Restaurant, atop Peachtree Tower, and prepared to spend two months' worth of entertainment budget on one meal. It was a big decision, but Liz deserved it. Besides, I was becoming attached to the woman who called almost daily to remind me of deadlines. The previous week, when she had only called twice, I found myself worrying if she'd given up on me.

The night of our dinner in the tower was cool and clear. The lights of Atlanta were sprinkled below us like stars that had fallen from the sky. Each time the floor rotated, and our table overlooked the Midtown area, we paused our meal to look for the space where the new landmarks of our project would stand.

Behind our conversation floated the Muzak version of old standards, most of them unremarkable. However, somewhere between the end of the main course and the appearance of dessert, the chords of "Yesterday," a Beatles' standard, drifted through the air. Having grown up a fan of the Fab Four, I was offended by the Muzak mélange that assaulted my memory. The offense was written all over my face when I looked up to see Liz in similar distress. It was then that I knew we were bound for a deeper relationship.

She supported me throughout the rest of the project, and I supported her dream of attending law school. Many weekends were spent with her ensconced on my sofa in jeans and one of my sweatshirts. By the time I had finished quizzing her from the study guides, I was confident I could have passed the LSAT. When Liz passed, we celebrated at one of the first restaurants to open in the Crossroads area. The years she spent in law school saw one of us burning up the road between Atlanta and Athens most weekends.

Valentine's Day in 1987 fell on a Saturday. Wanting to repeat the success of our first date, I reserved a table at The Sun Dial. If anything, Liz had taught me about Proper Prior Planning, and I was taking no chances of Piss Poor Performance, so I made my own flow chart.

January 2	Make Reservation for Valentine's Day
January 5	Visit bank for a loan
January 6	Buy a ring
February 2	Buy a new suit
February 7	Pick up the suit from tailor
February 14	Noon, Pick up a corsage
7:30 PM	Arrive at Sun Dial
Dessert	Place ring on finger

The evening was a success. Liz loved the ring, and together we set the date for the first Saturday in June. This way, we could honeymoon before she took the Bar in July. The partners at Howard, Angles & Linden, who had remembered the intern with a bent for dates, offered her a position to begin in August. The world was our oyster, and we were enjoying it together.

At least I thought we were. Abandoning your own 25th wedding anniversary doesn't say much for being happy together. Maybe I was wrong. Maybe Liz hasn't been happy.

I stop walking as a sob wracks my body. All I wanted was for her to be happy. I shake my head and breathe deeply. How could I have missed her unhappiness? Despondently, I drag myself towards the villa.

LIZ

"OK, kitty, out of the suitcase. I haven't got time to pet you. I've got a train to catch to Paris. Let's hope I've left enough time to get from the Gare de Lyon out to Charles de Gaulle." I toss Le Chat to the floor and return to the drawer for more clothes.

Undaunted, Le Chat jumps to the top of the dresser. Pacing the higher perch, she rubs against the mirror and the envelope propped there. Cat that she is, she paws at the envelope until it falls into the open drawer from which I am packing.

I lift the envelope from among the clothes and read the architecturally perfect print of my oldest son.

Open on June 6th.

That's tomorrow, and I won't be here. In a trance, I sink onto the bed and slide my finger under the flap. Inside, two sheets of elegant stationery. Carefully pulling them from the envelope, I read.

Mom & Dad

Happy 25th anniversary to THE BEST parents a guy could ask for! Because of you, I am living the life of my dreams. You taught me to dream big and never to give up. Thank you!

As Ashley and I prepare for our wedding, I think of the example you two set for Kyle and me. Thank you, Dad, for showing us that it's possible to have a successful career, be an active father, and support my wife's dreams at the same time. I hope I can live up to your example.

Mom, I am so proud of you and the work your firm has done for Atlanta. Not many women can claim to be a partner in an award-winning law firm, raise two wonderful boys--of which I am one--and be a loving wife.

You two are the best, and you deserve a long vacation far from the demands of everyday life. Drink plenty of wine, take time to watch the sunset, and let go of your responsibilities. This time is for you!

Love,

JR.

Tears stream down my face and onto the stationery. I watch as the paper's fibers absorb the salty drops.

Frantic barking from outside brings me back to the warm June morning. I step to the threshold of the window to find an old man below, carrying a box of vegetables. He is yelling at a dog in French - something about that old cat is all I can make out, high school French long behind me. As the old man looks up, I take a small step back. I don't want anyone seeing me in this condition.

Josh and Wendy join the old man and laugh as Le Chat haughtily walks the edge of the balcony railing, regally swishing her tail.

"You would think after all of these years, the two of them would become friends," Wendy observes.

Josh translates for the vegetable seller and takes the box from him, only to turn and hand it to Dave, who has joined the group in the garden.

"What's all the noise about, Chien?" Dave sets the box on the garden table and squats down. Chien trots over to Dave, who scratches his ear and chortles, gratuitous words of doggery—"Who's a good boy? Protecting your Pomme from that mean old cat?" The Americans laugh as the old man calls to the dog and turns to leave.

"I'll walk out with Pomme." As he turns, Josh speaks to Pomme. "Nous devons changer le menu pour le dîner de demain. "(We need to change the menu for tomorrow's dinner.)

I stand fixed in my position behind the curtains as Wendy wanders over to the large rosemary plant, seemingly searching for the perfect stem as Dave carries the box inside. When he returns, Dave watches Wendy wander through the herbs, taking in the dance of the bees among the ruffly purple flowers and inhaling the scent of the garden.

I watch as Wendy inhales the smell of the garden, her face glowing contentedly, a feeling I yearn for.

Dave smiles as he watches his wife meld with the landscape. "My only regret is that we didn't do this sooner. How could we have thought working 50 hours a week was so important?"

"I feel so at home here. It's as though the house was waiting for us to arrive."

"Dreams are that way, aren't they? We spent years dreaming of this life, and here it was when we came looking."

Josh comes around the side of the house. "I take it you're changing tomorrow's menu," says Dave.

"I have no idea what to feed a man with a broken heart, but I know it's definitely NOT the anniversary celebration he had dreamt of."

Dave squeezes Wendy's hand. "We all know that dreams are best when shared with the one you love." The three of them look towards the window and shake their heads before returning to the kitchen.

I feel a flush of anger run through me. What about MY dreams? I stomp my foot. Looking down, I find that one of my tears has high-lighted a section of Jr's letter,

'Partner in an award-winning law firm.'

"But there's so much more I can do!" Angrily, I shuffle the pages and find myself staring at a page written in sweeping calligraphy. A script that could only have been written by Kyle.

Mom & Dad,

What, you don't think I'm going to let Harris have the last word on this momentous day?

You know how I hate to repeat Harris, so believe me when I say "DITTO." And thanks for being great parents to both the nerdy math guy and me, your creative wanderer. We are off on our own adventures now, so it's time ya'll dream new dreams just for you.

Here's to finding your new Crossroads and enjoying the journey together.

Love,

Kyle

I crumple onto the edge of the bed. The truth settles over me. My boys don't need me. They are living their own lives. My work with them is done. But I wanted more time. There was so much I didn't get to do, and now they are off on their own.

I shake my head; "Harris and Ashley don't need help with their wedding, and Kyle would be horrified if I used my contacts in LA to make things happen. He'd think I didn't believe in him." A deep sigh escapes my lips as I collapse even further, my chin nearly touching my chest. Self-pity overwhelms me. "The years flew by, and I wasn't there. Harris carried such a big part of the load. He assured me everything would turn out fine, but now my boys are men, and there's no more time. What was I thinking?"

Atlanta will know I was here! I will be noticed!

They will know I made a difference!

They who? The city of Atlanta? Really? That's what I've worked for? They don't know me. And they don't care.

All my life, I've been smart, but not smart enough to win an award. I've been pretty, but not enough to be noticed. I've been the one who made sure the projects were successful. Did anyone notice? No, it was always the boss who went to the banquet. It was the boss who got the bonus. Even now, it's not me, it's the firm that got the award. Shaking my head, I try to clear the demons from my mind. What is wrong with me? I have a husband who loves me, my boys are happily independent, and I am a partner in an award-winning firm.

A knock on the door calls me back to the present. "Liz, we've got to get a move on if you want to catch the 11:00 AM train in Avignon."

I look about, suitcase half filled, tear-stained letters in my hand, and there sitting on the wall of the balcony, Le Chat—head cocked to one side as if to say, "Well?" Beyond Le Chat, the leaves of the willow tree sway against the azure sky as whisps of clouds blow by.

Enough! I'm done with these demons.

HARRIS & LIZ

Slipping through the front door, Harris quietly climbs the stairs. All he wants is a shower and to be alone. He has no desire to see pity in other people's faces or hear words of sympathy. He's feeling bad enough. He doesn't need to manage other people's feelings on top of it.

As Harris opens the door to the bedroom, he pulls his sweaty shirt over his head and turns toward the bathroom. From the corner of his eye, he catches the shape of someone in the room. He's not alone. He turns his body to focus. It's Liz! Stunned, happy, and perturbed at the same time, Harris freezes.

"I couldn't do it. I couldn't leave. I'm sorry I even thought about it. It took the words of two wise young men to bring me back to reality." Liz raises her hand, holding the tear-stained stationery. "I'm sorry. I opened our anniversary letter a day early."

Harris' joy takes the upper hand. In three quick steps, she is in his arms. "I have no idea what those boys had to say, but you can read my mail any time."

Liz collapses in tears in Harris' arms. Sobs wrack her body as he supports her. In his warm embrace, she feels safe and cared for. Her thoughts tumble in on her.

He has always been here for me. This is where I want to be, not some boardroom working for a client.

The feeling of her body relaxing into him softens Harris further. He can feel the old Liz. The Liz who opened her heart to him so many years ago. The woman who committed to sharing life with him. The partner who worked with him to make dreams come true. Harris is relieved to have her back.

Liz's tears run down Harris's chest until she can't breathe. Harris steps back, yanking tissues from the box on the dresser. When she blows her nose, they laugh, both of them remembering the elephant joke from the first time Liz had had a good cry in his arms. "Elephants never forget," they say together.

"I will never forget the first time I cried in your arms. You just let me cry. You didn't judge. You didn't try to solve my problems. You were just there. You have always been there for me. I love you and I want to be here for you."

Harris takes Liz in his arms again and holds her tight. "You are my light, Liz. You set visions that I can never imagine. You make me believe that we can accomplish them, and we do."

Liz feels Le Chat weaving between their legs. "It's all her fault. I wouldn't have even noticed the letter had she not knocked it into the drawer." Liz bends to scratch the cat behind the ears. Having been acknowledged, Le Chat jumps to the wall of the balcony and out to the tree limbs, disappearing into the foliage.

"And people think angels have wings. This one has whiskers."

"And an attitude, especially around the dog. You should have seen her."

Harris pulls Liz to him again. "I'm just happy she was here when the time was right. I love you, Liz. I always will."

An urgent knock at the door disrupts them. "Liz, I'm afraid we won't make the train. I'm not sure we can get to the station in time."

"I guess I should let them know that I'm staying." Liz steps to the door and opens it just a crack, hesitant to let Lee see her puffy face. "It's OK, Lee. I'll be staying. Harris and I have a lot to talk about. Thank you for the offer, though."

As the door closes, Lee steps back with a smile. "I knew she wouldn't leave. It just didn't feel right." Lee glances around as though looking for someone or something. Shrugging his shoulders, he heads down the stairs. "In this house, things always seem to work out the way they are meant to." Humming to himself, Lee bounces down the steps.

Harris tosses a big tip on the table as he and Liz finish lunch at the café in L'Esprit du Rhône. He doesn't care that people in France don't tip. He is feeling good and wants to share his joy. He and Liz decide to continue their conversation, so instead of turning in at the gate to Bonne Vie, they ramble down the road. Harris babbles on about the books he's been reading about life in France: the food, the wine, the light, the countryside. Liz listens to the lilt of his voice, but it is the happiness on Harris's face that strikes her most. He is euphoric. I haven't seen him like this since our honeymoon when we were dreaming of the life we would build together. Liz feels the armor she hadn't realized she was wearing slip away. The knot in her stomach has dissolved. She isn't worried about bringing Harris back to reality and the waiting list of tasks to be completed. His delight is infectious, and her heart is ready to share it.

The world around them feels new. They find themselves noticing small things that they'd missed over the previous two days—the heads of the sunflowers turning with the sun's path, helping them better appreciate their French name, tournesol,—"turn sun." Liz curtsies when Harris presents her with a small bunch of wildflowers. They while away the afternoon talking and laughing, like the couple they'd been 25 years earlier.

Liz is drawn to the rows of grape vines running parallel across the undulating fields. Looking at them is like watching soldiers march off to a distant battlefield. She wanders between the plants, appreciating the dark green leaves and the coiled tendrils that wrap around the wires holding the vines. Looking closely, she finds little bunches of pale green grapes, the beginning of this year's crop destined to become award-winning wines of the Côtes de Rhône. Now she wishes she'd paid more attention to Harris when he was reading to her from that stack of books he'd been studying. Liz pulls her cell phone from her pocket and begins snapping shots of the grapes from different angles. She loves the way the sun lights up the burgeoning little marbles, the shadows cast by the leaves, and the many different shades of green.

Backing away from her close-ups, she is drawn to the ancient vines, twisted and gnarled. She can see where the vines grow more smoothly and seem younger. Liz remembers watching part of a documentary with Harris where workers pruned vines back to small stumpy trees. This whole process is more interesting than I thought, she muses.

A loud, high-pitched shriek in what must be French startles Liz. She looks up to see a woman stalking toward her, red-faced, hands clenched, and a knife in one hand. She is screaming something in French.

Espions, vous êtes des espions. Ce sont Les Américains de la villa qui vous ont envoyé, n'est-ce pas ? Espions ! Espions ! Espions ! Espions !

The one word Liz hears over and over is espion. "Spy? Is she talking about me?"

Liz backs slowly down the row with her hands in front of her. "I'm sorry. We didn't mean to trespass. Your grapes are lovely. We just wanted to look at them. Really, we wouldn't hurt anything." The woman continues screaming, spit flying from her mouth, as she angrily backs Liz down the row. At the road, Harris grabs Liz's hand and pulls her away from the field. Together, they jog away from the crazy lady standing at the edge of the field, waving the knife and screaming.

As they round a bend in the road, the sound of the screaming lessens, and Liz and Harris slow to a walk. "What was that? She sounded as though you had taken an axe to the vines."

"I don't know. One minute I was lost among the vines, and the next I was being chased by a harpy. I guess technically we were trespassing, but really, all she had to do was ask."

Seeing that Liz is still shaken, Harris draws her close. "I guess we should say something to Wendy. Maybe she should let guests know to stay away from those fields."

Liz nods, still in shock from the confrontation.

Back at the villa, ensconced in one of the comfy patio chairs and sipping an Apéro spritz, Liz shares her experience with their hosts. She shakes her head in disbelief. "For years I've walked the streets of Atlanta vigilant of attack, and it's here among the grapes in Provence that this happens. That woman. She was literally spitting mad. I was afraid she was going to attack me."

Wendy leans towards Liz and squeezes her hand. "I'm sorry. We knew Camille was a bit strange, but we never thought she'd be aggressive. None of our previous guests have reported anything like this. We'll have to include warnings to stay out of the grapes in our welcome package. Ugh, Welcome to L'Esprit du Rhône, home of the best wines of the Côtes de Rhône. Now, stay away from the grapes!

"Remember that day she came to talk to me about NOT making wine from our grapes? It was the strangest conversation. Do you think Camille thought Liz was taking photos for us? Not that we'd know what we were looking at. I mean, the grapes are beautiful, and Josh did make some interesting jelly with them last year." Lee makes a face remembering the taste. It was nothing like the grape jelly he'd grown up with, much less the taste he'd been expecting. Thankfully, Josh used most of the jelly as part of his hors d'oeuvres, and Lee was able to switch to apricot jam.

"I think there's more to it," muses Dave. "From what I've been picking up at the café, Camille and her father were never fans of Monsieur and Madame. Her hostility may have more to do with the house than anything else."

"That's weird. For me, the experience has been exactly the opposite. When someone realizes I'm from Bonne Vie, it's like they fall all over themselves to be helpful," remarks Josh. "I even thought it might be helpful to have polo shirts made with the name Bonne Vie on them. Has anyone seen a coat of arms for Monsieur?"

"Funny you should say that. Someone at the café was talking about Monsieur's bloodline last year. But André shut down the conversation, saying Monsieur never asked for special treatment while he was alive, so there's no need for that conversation now that he's gone. I tell you, André may seem like an affable old man, but he's a strict ring master in that café of his."

Everyone sits silently, lost in thought. Each has experienced a different piece of the puzzle—the grapes, Camille, André, the villa,

Monsieur, and a legacy that isn't quite clear to these newcomers. The pieces connect like the threads of a spider's web; disturb one, and they all shimmer in the fading light of the past.

13

Matching Problems to Solutions

Ah, pastis, I have earned this respite. After warming my stomach, your heat has seeped through the rest of my body. Throbbing feet and tightly wound back muscles are but a small price to pay for the success of this day. The meal has been served, and the crowd is enjoying the band. Another joyful Bastille Day celebration is drawing to a close. Weary body, you betray my youthful heart that yearns to join the children scurrying between the tables and splashing in the fountain, as I did when Papa and Maman served the holiday meal. My legs may no longer allow me to race about and play in the water, but every year I eagerly anticipate this day filled with friends, music, and fireworks. There will never be too many Bastille Days!

Papa believed life was meant to be joyful and that God brought happiness to those who were happy. He often told me, "Not all of life's successes are due to hard work. Sometimes serendipity and earthly angels are responsible. And for those, we must be grateful." For Maman and Papa, the serendipity was Monsieur falling in love with Madame who refused to leave the Vaucluse. Although his love for Madame embraced her and the town, the town was slow to adopt him. Papa felt for the tall, lanky man who quietly sipped his daily coffee at the café before heading to the bank to check on business with

Monsieur De La Cour, the bank manager. So, Papa made a point to say a few friendly words and ask after Monsieur & Madame's health. Although their interactions were brief, Papa felt it was important that the gentleman be noticed. One morning in 1931, a month before my birth, Papa failed to engage Monsieur in usual pleasantries, causing the thoughtful man to wonder what was amiss. While visiting with Monsieur De La Cour at the bank that morning, Monsieur wondered aloud about his friend Monsieur Durand.

"Monsieur Durand seemed preoccupied this morning, not his usual friendly self."

"Oui, I imagine he was thinking of the stove that needs replacing. Monsieur Durand was here yesterday to request a loan. Unfortunately, he does not hold the deed for his building, and the business has no assets. They barely get by from one month to the next. I am sorry to say he did not qualify for such a loan."

"Hmm…Madame Durand is quite heavy with child, is she not?"

"Yes, Madame De La Cour tells me she is expected to give birth next month."

"Draw up the loan and have the stove delivered to Monsieur Durand. A man whose work is led by happiness will find a way to make good on his word."

And so, Monsieur became the earthly angel who blessed our café with a stove and me with a warm home into which to be born.

A giggling child bumps into my table, bringing me back to the celebration. Savoring another draught from my cup, I consider this new pastis and am glad Jacques suggested it when he delivered my last order. I must let Claude know that I will be purchasing a case. He'll need to make space for it in the cellar.

Laughter erupts at a table across the walk. Papa was right, life is a joy. Today we sold out of champagne. Looks like we'll need to keep more on hand again. There hasn't been much call for it since the crash in '08. But I have a feeling people are ready to enjoy themselves again.

I feel someone above me.

"Maman says you need to drink a bottle of this with your pastis. You've had a long day, and we'd hate for you to miss the fireworks. They're your favorite part of the celebration."

Chloé sets a bottle of sparkling water and a glass on the table before kissing me on the cheek and returning to her work. Chuckling, I wonder if this newest feeling of contentment is due to the new pastis or Chloe's kiss.

What a wonderful young lady Chloé has grown into. She is yet another dividend from the favor I did for Monsieur so many years ago. When I agreed to help him solve a problem for a friend from Dijon, I had no idea how much happiness it would bring me. But of course, Monsieur knew. He always knew how to match solutions to problems in a way that benefited both parties. He seemed to have a sixth sense about people. A sense that I like to feel I have learned from him.

I remember that day. It was fall, and the first cold Mistral had blown in. Lingering over his coffee that morning until the early crowd had dwindled, I knew Monsieur had something on his mind.

"André, would you consider taking on a full-time employee? I know a young man who needs a new beginning."

"I hadn't thought of hiring anyone just yet."

We looked up as Yvette set a cup of coffee before me and moved on to another table.

"Nice girl. She's done a good job of taking care of customers. I wasn't going to look for a replacement until spring when her baby comes. I suppose I could take on a replacement early."

After years of working with Monsieur, I knew not to second-guess his intentions, and I was sure I could find something to keep the young man busy until Yvette gave birth.

The first few days, Claude cleaned tables, swept floors, and washed dishes while Yvette and I went about our business. As days went on,

Claude quietly restocked the bar and kitchen without being asked. Yvette and I felt a sense of relief from these more laborious tasks and gratefully settled into a new routine.

On the 25th of each month, I visited the small closet I called a storeroom to prepare the dry goods order. What used to be a jumble of items had become neat rows of foodstuffs, lines of paper goods, and, hidden behind the door, cleaning items. Turning to take in the changes, I knocked into a clipboard hanging on the wall. On it was a list of items stored in the room with checks next to the name of each item. Stunned, I walked to the bar where Claude was making coffee.

"I like what you've done in the storeroom. It makes ordering easier."

"Each time I remove an item from the closet, I check it off. I don't know what was there before I arrived, but I can tell you exactly what has been used since I organized it."

I hadn't needed to find anything to keep the boy busy; he'd figured it out for himself.

As the days shortened, Yvette's child grew, and her pace slowed. When the café became busy, and it looked as though she might fall behind, Claude quietly delivered food and drinks to tables. In a short time, he had learned the habits of the regulars and had their orders ready by the time Yvette made her way to the bar. Claude's observance and efficiency made the shift between the two smooth and natural. It was as though the boy had grown up in the café.

The following summer, Monsieur dallied over his cup once again.

"You and Claude seem to be doing well."

"Oui, merci Monsieur. You supplied me with a solution before I was even aware there was a problem."

"I prefer to see this pairing as the joining together of family members who were inadvertently born in different parts of the country."

"So, it seems."

"Would you mind if I gift the young man an education?"

"But of course! Claude is too bright not to use that brain of his."

Monsieur's wise eyes probed mine as a wan smile crossed his lips.

"Your words say yes, my friend, but your eyes betray you."

I shifted my weight from one foot to the other and looked away.

"I admit I've become attached to the boy. I wish only the best for him, but I would hate to see him leave."

"I have a feeling the bond is mutual. I'm pretty sure the life he chooses after his degree will keep him nearby."

Before long, Claude had decided that courses at the University of Avignon would be right for him. He wanted to study business. With each course he took, we both learned new ways to strengthen the café's finances. Together we worked to cut unnecessary expenses, began a savings account for "capital" expenses, and eventually took out a loan to remodel the kitchen and living area above the café. When Claude graduated, it turned out that the only opportunity he was interested in kept him in L'Esprit du Rhône and close to Désirée, whom he had met at university. The new apartments were completed just before Claude and Désirée married. A year later, Chloé entered our lives, completing our happy family. Once again, Monsieur had serendipitously brought warmth into my life.

A rollicking American country song shakes me from my rêverie. The square is filled with people, and everyone is enjoying the music in both French and English. I haven't been keeping track, but it does seem there are more English songs this year. I wonder if Josh's smiling requests have anything to do with that. The villa's table is full. Not only have the four of them come to celebrate with us, but Wendy's family is here as well as a few guests. It's nice to see the big house full of life again.

And thanks to Josh, Pomme has returned to the celebration. For the past few years, he'd been telling me his old ears couldn't handle the noise, but I suspect it was the dread of walking home after a full day of celebration that had kept him away. Between Margot's insistence and Josh's offer of a ride, his "old ears" seem to have improved.

Not only have his ears improved, but the bounce in his step has returned, and when he laughs, it's from his belly like when we were young. When his laughter fills the air, I look for that dark-eyed girl he loved and remember the days when the four of us would slip away for picnics near the river—Pomme with Lizette and me with my Marie. My heart tightens, and I tightly squeeze my eyes to keep the bittersweet memories from slipping out. Oh, Marie, another Bastille Day without you, and we had promised one another that we would spend every holiday together for the rest of our lives. We were sure we were meant to be, but your father refused to release an old family grudge—the original insult no longer remembered. Your father forbade you from becoming a Durand and sent you away to the Dordogne even before we had finished school.

Determined to find you and take you to a place where old feuds had no meaning, I finished school, saved my francs, and waited patiently. When I was ready, I asked Papa if Monsieur would help me find you. After too many sleepless nights, the heartbreaking answer came. You were gone, not only from L'Esprit du Rhône, but from this Earth. They said you had died of pneumonia that winter in those frigid mountains far from the one who loved you. But I believe it was a broken heart that made you give up on life. I would never hear your teasing words or feel your warm touch again. I was crushed and knew my heart would never love again. There was no place to go, so I stayed in L'Esprit du Rhône, living one day after another in a trance, until Monsieur asked for a favor.

The day the favor was requested was like the others. Monsieur settled into his usual table, but this time Papa asked me to deliver his coffee. That should have been a sign that something was about to happen. Papa always waited on Monsieur.

"Good morning, André."

Monsieur's greeting awakened me from my trance. We had never really spoken before, and in that second, I realized Monsieur was there to see me.

"Bonjour, Monsieur."

Nodding my head, I gently set his cup on the table and looked into his warm, searching eyes. I felt the need to say something. What was it that Papa and he talked about each morning? What should I be saying to this man whom we all knew of, but who was a stranger beyond his quiet presence?

"Yes, you are correct. I have come to speak with you."

How did he know what I was thinking?

"I would like to request a favor of you."

Me? What could I possibly do for this rich and important man? But yes. I did owe him a favor. It wasn't his fault that the news his man brought back broke my heart. I was honor-bound to meet his request.

"Oui, Monsieur. How can I be of service?"

"My friend Emile is taking a trip to Paris and needs a strong young man to help him with his package. He is having problems getting around just now, and I would appreciate your seeing that he and the package make it on and off the train."

"Oui, Monsieur," I nodded. His friend, Emile? I thought Monsieur stole Madame from Emile. The story Emile's brother, Lucas, tells is that Monsieur was the bane of the Roche family. But Monsieur claims Emile as his friend and wants me to help him.

"Merci, André. If you could meet Monsieur Roche at the train station tomorrow morning at 7:00, I would be grateful. Monsieur Roche will have your ticket, and I'm sure he will see that you have a nice meal while the two of you are in Paris."

The next morning, I stood stomping my feet to circulate the blood in my toes, the cold seeping up from the damp ground. Eventually, a farm truck pulled up carrying Emile Roche. A worker from the vineyard stepped out to retrieve a package from the bed of the truck. Handing me the package, he nodded at Monsieur Roche and left.

"Bonjour, André."

"Bonjour, Monsieur."

As we made our way to the ticket window, I found myself following a man whose movements would have one guess his age to be well beyond his 46 years. His legs moved slowly, as though they needed urging to take each step, and his shoulders slumped beneath the weight of an invisible burden. This was not the man I knew Emile Roche to be. He had always been active and vibrant, a man who walked his fields daily and reveled in each sunrise. Whatever had happened, I now understood why Monsieur had asked me to accompany him.

On the platform, we waited for the train to arrive. Emile gazed across the tracks, lost in thought. Occasionally, his eyes would glisten, and he would squeeze them shut, shaking his head as though to banish thoughts that haunted him. Finally, the train arrived. Entering the car, I moved to place the package on the luggage rack above our seats. A look of panic passed across Emile's face.

"I don't think the train will be crowded this morning. The package will be fine on the seat beside you."

We sat in facing seats, with me on the aisle, the package on the window seat, and Emile across from it, ever mindful of its safety. I now had time to consider just what it was that I was transporting. It was not the case of wine I had expected. This package was as long as my arm and almost as wide, but less than half a meter deep. Through the paper, I could feel the edges of a wooden box. The question was what was within the box. Although hefty, its weight was not burdensome. Not bottles of wine or paperwork that needed to be signed. A new sign for the gate of the vineyard? But he would not be taking that to Paris.

Monsieur Roche spent the trip looking from the package to the French countryside and back, his mind far from the Paris-bound train. Eventually, the rocking of the car and the rhythmic sound of the tracks lulled me in and out of a dozing sleep. I awoke as the train slowed for the station. Monsieur Roche rose and placed his hat on his head.

"Come, André, we will take a cab to our destination."

Retrieving the package, I followed the somber man.

Monsieur Roche asked that I sit in the front of the cab so that the package could rest on the seat next to him.

"Ministère de la Culture, s'il te plaît."

Now I was confused. Ministère de la Culture? Yes, wine is an essential part of the French culture, but I'm pretty sure the Ministère de l'Agriculture oversees that.

My mind whirled as I watched our progress along the Seine, passing Notre Dame and the Louvre. I willed myself to pay attention to my surroundings and not waste this opportunity. I was in Paris, the capital of the country and the center of world culture. Yes, the center of culture, and we were headed directly to the Ministère de la Culture, a stone's throw from the Louvre.

When the driver opened the door for Monsieur Roche, I grabbed the package from the rear seat and followed him inside.

"Bonjour. The office of Monsieur Laurent?"

"Bonjour, first floor, number 4, to the right at the top of the stairs."

"Merci."

Monsieur Roche walked across the foyer and slowly began the climb. His movements were labored as he struggled to lift one foot after the other. He moved as though he were a man sentenced to the guillotine instead of a wealthy vineyard owner visiting the Ministère de la Culture in Paris.

"Bonjour. I am here to see Monsieur Laurent. He is expecting me."

"Bonjour, Monsieur Roche. Oui, Monsieur Laurent is expecting you. One moment, please."

The secretary rose, knocked on Monsieur Laurent's door, and opened it.

"Monsieur Roche is here."

A voice called "Merci, Sara," as the secretary opened the door wider. Monsieur Laurent greeted Monsieur Roche. Spying the package under my arm, he pointed across the room.

"Please, place the painting on the table."

I carefully deposited my paper-wrapped ward on the flat surface.

"You may wait in the outer office with my secretary."

Monsieur Laurent nodded his head towards the chairs along the wall across from the secretary's desk.

I took a seat as thoughts whirled in my mind. What is going on? Why are we here? What painting was that, and why has Monsieur Roche not spoken of it?

My thoughts were disturbed by the entrance of a gentleman dressed in a grey flannel suit.

"Bonjour. I am Monsieur Dupont from the Louvre. I am here to review the painting for Monsieur Laurent."

"Bonjour. Yes, please go right in."

The gentleman nodded as he walked to the door and gently knocked before entering.

I heard muffled greetings and introductions as the door closed.

I knew the Roche family was well-off, but I didn't realize they owned art that the Ministère de la Culture and the Louvre would be interested in.

As I pondered the situation, the phone rang, and I half-heartedly listened to the secretary's conversation.

"Oui, Monsieur Laurent has signed those papers. The Brugge tapestries will soon be ready for transfer. No, the Courbet landscapes are not ready yet. Yes, I know, but the art from Munich was immense. It will take a long time before we can process everything. "

Business in the office swirled around me as I gathered pieces of the story of this place and tried to understand just what was in the package I had carried for Monsieur Roche. After an hour, the door to Monsieur Laurent's office opened, as "thank you's and "goodbyes" were said before the old man turned to me.

"I believe I owe you a lunch for your service, André."

As I descended the steps behind Monsieur Roche, I noticed a change. His shoulders were straighter, and his legs moved in a gait more normal for a man of his age. It was as though a great weight had been lifted from him. And in fact, his energy was more buoyant.

At the front walk, we stopped. Monsieur Roche took in his surroundings as though he had not stood in the spot an hour earlier.

"It is quite a nice day. I think we shall walk to lunch. This way, my boy."

Half an hour later, I found myself sitting across the table from a changed man. The brisk walk seemed to have completed the transformation of the earlier troubled man, and he was once more Emile Roche, vintner and connoisseur of fine foods.

Speaking to the waiter, "Ah, Yves, your agneau, please." "Their lamb is very nice, André, you may want to try it." Turning back to the waiter. "And a bottle of our Rèves Perdus, please."

I nodded in agreement, and Yves left to retrieve a bottle of Maison Roche's finest.

"Yves was the first to serve our wines in his restaurant here in Paris. I like to return the favor by dining here whenever I am in town."

I nodded again as thoughts of the morning swirled in my mind. I had no idea what to say, nor could I find the words to ask the questions I wanted answered.

"I see you are preoccupied with the events of this morning. I appreciate your patience and trust. I cannot tell you everything, but I will say that this trip has removed a great burden from my shoulders."

Before I could stop myself, I blurted, "And the painting?"

Looking away for a moment, Emile breathed deeply. Returning to my gaze he exhaled and began.

"Of course, you've had time to put the pieces together. Yes, you delivered a valuable painting to Monsieur Laurent's office this morning. Not long ago, I discovered it at Mason Roche. It appears to have been a gift from a German associate of my brother's during the war. Lucas knew I would disapprove and kept it from me. Once I discovered its existence, I began the process of returning it to its rightful owner. Today we delivered the painting to people who will see that it once again hangs on the walls of the family from which it was taken."

The thoughts in my mind were a maelstrom. A gift from a German associate? But the Roches would never work with the Germans. I may have been young, but I remember how proud everyone at Maison Roche was of Mario going off to fight when Britain joined France to stop the German invasion. Everyone said how proud the old man would have been of Mario's defending of La République. The Roches were no fans of Germany, especially after Richard Roche lost his brother in the Battle of Verdun in World War I.

But when Mario returned, things didn't go well for him at Maison Roche. Lucas said Mario didn't want to work anymore. Mario wouldn't talk about it, and not long after their last disagreement, Mario disappeared. Maybe there was more to the story than Mario's not wanting to work. Perhaps it wasn't the work, but who he was working for.

But no, Emile would never go along with that. He knew how his father felt about the Germans. Something else was going on. What agreements had Lucas made behind Emile's back? But really, a Roche working with Germans?

Ah, then again, Lucas was a different Roche. The old man and Emile were always smiling and had a kind word for everyone they passed. Lucas, on the other hand, seemed to carry a black cloud with him—no smile, no nod of acknowledgement, not even the obligatory bonjour. It was as though he resented having to live among us ordinary folks. He rarely came to the café and seldom spoke to anyone outside of the vineyard. When he did, his words were tainted with bitterness and distrust. Few people had anything to do with him, and he seemed to like it that way. Yes, I can see how Lucas may have gotten mixed up with the Germans.

A memory passes through my mind. Mario's mother's funeral! A contingent of German soldiers arrived in town just in time for the funeral and stayed for a month. None of us knew what had happened to Mario, but there had been talk of how much he hated the Germans and what the Vichy government was doing to the country. Had he joined the Résistance? Did Lucas share his suspicions with the Germans? Had they come to L'Esprit du Rhône hoping to arrest Mario?

I looked up to find Emile calmly observing me, giving me time to draw the only conclusion he knew there was to draw. Emile had had to deal with the collaborator living in his own house. He had carried the shame it brought to his family. And today he was able to release part of that weight.

I looked back at Emile.

"I am happy my favor for Monsieur was of service to you, Monsieur Roche. I hope the painting finds its way back home."

Emile smiled softly. "Arnoux knew what he was doing when he suggested you accompany me today. He is a wise man, and I am grateful to call him a friend."

Arnoux? Most of us don't even know Monsieur's first name, much less refer to him by it. They really must be friends. But the story Lucas shares is much different. He claims Monsieur's stealing of Madame from Emile was an insult that could not be forgiven, and that Monsieur cannot be trusted. Ah, but then again, that is the way Lucas would see it. Lucas has never understood love. True love wishes the beloved nothing but happiness. If Emile truly loved Madame, all he would want was her happiness.

I surreptitiously wipe the tears from my eyes as my mind returns to the celebration around me. Oh, so many years have passed since that first favor. It wasn't too many years later that Maman died, and soon after, I took Papa's place as Monsieur's partner in matching problems to their solutions. How I miss Papa and Monsieur. Together, they cared for the people of the community. A few of the recipients understood their luck, but many never made the connection, and that was fine with Monsieur. He only wished happiness for those around him. When he found Madame, he found his peace and his place in the world. He didn't need more than that.

Now Monsieur is but a memory, and his magic has faded. Yet something new is in the air. A new magic emanates from the villa these days. Pomme and Margot have come together. Fabien has returned to the garden of his heart, and Gérard has brought life back to the bubbling fountain at the villa. Just maybe, the ember of magic left by Monsieur and Madame is catching fire once again.

14

Nothing to Do and No One to Do it With

NATE, AUGUST 2012

I FEEL LIKE I'VE BEEN DUMPED OUT OF A ROLLED-UP CARPET AFTER being hauled cross- country in the back of a van, not delivered to Paris in a business class seat on Air France. My college roommate, Mark, wasn't joking when he said the trip from Jersey to L'Esprit du Rhône would be a long haul. Yesterday, I got up before the sun to catch the shuttle to JFK. Then, I boarded an Air France flight to Charles De Gaulle. Bleary-eyed from the overnight trip, I wandered around the luggage belts looking for my bag. I hadn't been crazy about the bright orange X Sarah taped to my brand-new suitcase, but when it flashed from the sea of identical black cases, I was tempted to dance.

Luggage in hand, I set out to find the train station in this city that calls itself an airport. The challenge was easier than I expected, so I treated myself to coffee and a croissant. The flaky pastry melting in my mouth, followed by the bitter, hot liquid, reminded me why I let myself be talked into this trek. Fueled by caffeine and butter, I headed back to the station to wait for my train to Avignon. It was a good time to pull out the book my daughter had given me for the trip—Peter Mayle's Year in Provence. "Dad, not everything there is to know about France can be found in a history book." All I could do was shrug. What did she expect of her father, the history professor?

My head bumped against the window, waking me from my nap. There's something about the rhythmic sound of the tracks that engages a sleep-deprived mind. Try as I might to stay awake, I spent the three-hour trip drifting in and out of sleep.

Saying I was overwhelmed with joy to see Dave would be an understatement. We've never been close, so I'm sure the hug I gave him was a surprise. My exhausted body gave me two choices: hug or collapse. Turns out he understood.

"Don't worry, you'll be as good as new after one of Josh's pick-me-ups. He's revived many a weary traveler. You know the trans-Atlantic travel rule: no sleeping before the sun goes down, or your body clock will be even more screwed up."

Groaning, I followed Dave to the car. I was about to drift off again, but the first thing Dave did was drive past the city walls and along the river. Avignon's history captured my attention! I wanted to learn more. Then Dave crossed the river and headed through the countryside. The scenery was less stunning than the ancient buildings, but in the August sun, the hazy lavender and sunflower fields enchanted me.

Now, sitting in the garden, drink in hand and savoring Josh's post-travel snacks, I've decided that Josh is my new best friend. That man's pick-me-up cocktail mixes the buzz of strong espresso with the kick of good vodka, and his appetizers surpass airplane food, even Air France's front-of-the-plane menu. I know things could have been worse if I hadn't let Mark talk me into upgrading my travel status.

Nate, what are you saving your money for? Enjoy your vacation! Get yourself a business class seat. Eat well, have a few drinks, and sleep. You'll arrive in Paris ready to enjoy France.

Great plan. I purchased the business class seat. I ate well and enjoyed some excellent wine, but did I sleep? No. Instead, I watched movies. They were titles I'd heard about over the past two years but hadn't made the effort to see. Was it curiosity that drew me in, or fear of sleeping and the dreams that come with it?

It's been nearly two years since Andrea died. We had plans for our retirement. Andrea created one of those vision boards, filled with pictures of the places we wanted to visit. We dreamed of traveling the world, meeting new people, walking the streets of ancient cities (my contribution to the list), and learning more about ourselves (Andrea's dream of spending time in an ashram). That balloon burst the day the aneurysm in her brain did.

Aneurysm? Burst? Nothing Gary tried to explain made sense. Andrea was one of the healthiest women I'd ever known—good diet, yoga every morning, hiking or biking every weekend.

Andrea worked in Gary's medical office. She coordinated both the medical and business sides of his operation for 20 years. There aren't many RNs with master's degrees in business. Gary recognized the asset he had in Andrea, and his appreciation for her work was one reason she waited so long to retire. That afternoon, Andrea complained of a headache and decided to leave early. She never made it home. She collapsed in the parking lot next to her car. By the time they found her, she was gone.

That was early December. The girls came home for the funeral; my colleagues took over my classes for the rest of the semester, and my world slowed to a dull gray. Eventually, everyone went back to their routines, and so did I. The University suggested I take the winter semester off to get my life in order. What life? What order? There was nothing to do and no one to do it with, so I stepped back onto the well-worn path of a tenured university professor. History is being made every day, but what I teach didn't require anything new of me, so I dusted off my notes and kept on marching.

I taught that winter semester, both summer sessions, and the entire following year. If there was a class to teach, I was your guy. Teaching history was familiar. I knew where I was and what to expect. There were no decisions to make. Life was simple.

The girls worried about me. They told me I needed to branch out and try something different. I told them, "There's nothing to do and no one to do it with." This spring, they decided I needed a vacation. I needed to get out of New Jersey, and no, my monthly visits to the city for dinner with my youngest daughter, Sarah, didn't count. They invited me to join Miriam and her family for their annual retreat to

North Carolina. She informed me that their third bedroom wasn't spoken for yet and was mine for the taking. Nothing about two weeks in a beach house with my semi-orthodox son-in-law sounded good to me. He is the perfect husband for Miriam and a great dad to Ruth, but Levi and I have absolutely nothing in common. Getting through a Thanksgiving weekend with him exhausts me.

I told the girls I would come up with something. There must be some historic sites in New England I hadn't covered. I could take a road trip around Massachusetts, which would count as getting out of Jersey.

Soon after the girls' ultimatum, Mark called to brag about his spring break in France. "We finally got to visit Susan's sister Wendy and her husband Dave in their French villa. It's in this wonderful little town called L'Esprit du Rhône. And get this, their place is called Bonne Vie – Good Life!" Mark rattled on about the house, the food, the wine, and the people who live there. Mark and I have been sharing travel stories since we were roommates in college. I always opted for the historical sites; he was more interested in the literary venues. As we've aged, his travels have shifted toward a newfound interest in wine. I, on the other hand, have continued to let history guide my travels. "You really should go, Nate. You know Wendy and Dave. They'd love to have you."

"I don't know, Mark, Andrea used to handle all our travel arrangements." I had made that sad realization once I figured out I didn't have a navigator for my road trip in Massachusetts. "Going all the way to France is a lot of work. The kind I have no experience with."

"Get your passport updated, and Susan and I will tell you which flight to take from JFK and the connecting train to Avignon. Dave will pick you up from the station, and the rest is easy. Throw some clothes in a bag, a few of those history books you like, and get ready to relax. "

It's August, and I've made the trip. The garden looks beautiful. I am being well-fed and watered. The girls might have been right; I needed to get out of New Jersey.

"Quit being a hermit. Get out and meet people. Enjoy yourself."

"But there's nothing to do and no one to do it with."

"Stop that, Nate. There's a world to discover and people just waiting to meet you." Andrea's voice echoes in my dreams. I roll over as she pushes me toward the edge of the bed.

Opening my eyes, I realize the sun is rising. Tears well up, and I stifle a sob. Andrea visits my dreams. I know because I have vague memories of talking to her. It's only when I wake from a dream that I remember specifics. Her message is always the same: get out there and live life. She doesn't understand. I miss her so much. She was always the one who pulled me from my books and involved me in the world. She was my guide. Without Andrea, there's nothing to do and no one to do it with. Just thinking those words, I can feel her pushing me to get out of bed.

I've come all this way; I might as well get up and explore Provence. I may have a PhD in American History, but I have much to learn about France, its Roman roots, and the scars left by the Germans—no sense missing out on the opportunity to learn something new.

"See, I told you there was something to do." I hear Andrea in my thoughts.

I wander down to the kitchen where someone is moving about.

"Morning, Wendy!"

"Hi, Nate. Sorry if I woke you. I usually try to get the coffee ready and put croissants in the oven before our guests rise."

"Don't worry, it wasn't you that woke me. I heard the birds." No use sharing my woes.

"Morning, Nate." Dave pats my back as he enters the kitchen. "I know you went down early last night, but I wasn't expecting to see you up at dawn your first morning."

"It was the birds," Wendy tells Dave. Turning back to me, she says, "In the summer, we sleep with the windows open, no need for an alarm clock. The birds know when it's time to get up."

Dave laughs, "Yeah, it's one of the perks of life in the Provence. Like coffee at André's. Want to join me?"

"You sure you want to drag Nate to your French lesson his first morning here?"

"The morning crowd at André's isn't just a French lesson; it's how I stay connected to the town. I've learned more about life around here from my time at the café than I would from reading a newspaper. Plus, after two years, I've become part of the ensemble. They'd wonder what happened to me if I didn't show up."

"I'm not sure how much college French I remember, but coffee sounds good."

"Oh, and Andre's croissants are divine." Patting his belly, Dave chuckles to himself. "Take my word for it. I've had one every morning since I began my French lessons."

Eyes look up, and a few heads nod in acknowledgment as Dave leads the way to a table near the fountain. "This is my regular summer spot. I've tried them all, except the ones that were already taken—there were a few old-timers here before me." Dave winks at me. "From here I can watch the sun as it rises over the buildings and eventually lights up the water of the fountain."

An ancient man with large hands quietly sets a croissant and a cup of coffee in front of Dave.

Turning to me, he says, "Bonjour, ami de Dave."

"Bonjour," I respond, remembering basic French etiquette.

"Comment aimerais-tu commencer ta journée?"

I turn to Dave questioningly. "He wants to know what you want."

"The same, merci." I nod towards Dave's food.

"Merci, André," Dave says. The old man nods as he leaves.

"Wow! That's a big guy, and scarily quiet."

"I guess so. We have an understanding. I practice my French with André, and we both act like he doesn't understand English. Most importantly, he doesn't let on that I understand more French than I seem to."

"That's lots of pretending going on."

"Yeah, but it works. I get to listen in on the gossip without anyone knowing I understand, and André doesn't upset his regulars by acting more worldly than they'd like. It's all about keeping things French."

My coffee and croissant are quietly placed in front of me as André moves on to serve other customers.

Dave looks at me with understanding eyes. "I know you were pushed into this trip. Don't know if you have any plans or a wish list, but let me know if there is anything you'd like to see. With Josh and Wendy preoccupied with running the villa, and Lee busy helping other American expats remodel the old houses they've purchased, I've got plenty of time on my hands. I can take you wherever you'd like to go. We've been here for over two years, and there are still places I haven't been. You know, history goes back thousands of years here; that's at least 10 times what we have in the States."

"I've read about the amphitheater and the arch in Orange, and there's the arena in Nîmes. Pont du Gard looks interesting, too. But you piqued my interest yesterday when we drove past the walls of Avignon. There's a Palace of the Popes there, isn't there? And that quirky bridge to nowhere, of course."

"Avignon might be a good choice for today. It's close. Orange is closer, but you really want to wait until Thursday to go there. We can visit the market and then do some sightseeing. Hmm, maybe not. Wendy will want to bring food home and not stick around. We'll see if we can work something out with Josh. That way we can take two cars. We can all go to the market, and afterwards you and I can stick around for the sights." Dave glances around and notices a discussion at a nearby table. "Pardon me while I gaze at the water for a while." Leaning towards me, he whispers, "I want to tune in on today's gossip." Smiling, his eyes glaze over as he leans back and stares at the fountain.

This gives me time to take in the town center. Besides the flashing green neon pharmacy sign, this place looks like a set for an old movie.

OK, there are new cars on the streets, but the storefronts are original, from what, the 1860s? People come and go from the boulangerie and boucher—words whose meaning comes to mind as I watch shoppers with their arms full of packages. Customers at the café have come and gone, some tossing down their espresso and moving on, while others linger to check on each other's news of the day. The fountain is indeed beautiful, larger than the fountain at the villa, but its song is nowhere as melodic. I lean back and let the sun's rays warm my face. My eyes close, and I drift off.

Dave's voice cuts through the background buzz. "Are we going off to Avignon this morning, or would you rather nap?"

Sitting upright in my chair, I tilt my cup back to ensure I've drained every bit of caffeine. "Let's hit the road! I didn't come all this way just to sleep. Enchant me with your history, Avignon!"

Dave leaves a 5 Euro note on the table, and we head back to the villa. Once we're out of earshot, he leans in and says, "You wouldn't believe what Yvette's daughter told her husband."

I laugh to myself, thinking small towns all over the world are the same, no matter the language.

Provence's morning music drifts through my foggy mind. I gradually become aware of the bed that surrounds me. I have slept peacefully through the night, with no confusing feelings of grasping at dreams. This morning, no force urges me out of bed. I am…happy, content.

Stretching, I rearrange myself to look through the French doors. The sun's light is just beginning to peek above the horizon, and I think to myself, today's story is yet to be written. Memories of the past few days drift through my mind— a tour of Palais du Papes, a perfect poulet rôti at a local café free from tourists, and the August sun shimmering in the sky as we returned to the villa. Swaying in Lee's hammock in the shade of the orchard, Josh waking me from my nap to ask if I'd like to join them for an amuse-bouche and apéritif before the meal. Laughing at the table afterward, while this merry group of newly minted Francophiles shared stories of their new lives in L'Esprit du Rhône. Once again, I realize how content I feel—I could get used to this. Looking out the window again, I see it's time to get up and prepare for today's French lesson. I hop out of bed, ready to enjoy my day.

"Dave, I've been thinking of taking in more recent history while I'm here. One of my fellow history professors gave me some pages from a manuscript he's reviewing for a friend. His friend's thesis is on the survival of the Jews in France during World War II. It seems, unlike other European countries, the Jews of France survived at much higher rates than those further east.

Interestingly, since the French Revolution in the 1790s, Jews have been regarded as citizens of France. To the French, Jews were citizens who simply practiced the faith of Israel. Before World War II, the average French person didn't pay much attention to their neighbor's religion. The fact that someone's grandfather fought in World War I was more significant than their religion. Liberté, Égalité, Fraternité are more than just words for the French, and anyone willing to fight for those words, Jew or not, was considered a Frenchman."

Dave nods, "Interesting, I didn't know that."

"There's a place called Les Milles somewhere north of Marseille where they interned people they'd rounded up when the war with Germany broke out in '39—foreigners, many of them German Jews, some dissidents. When the Vichy government took over, they worked with the Germans to continue the process. Some of those interned managed to get visas to other countries, some escaped, and a large number died from disease, mainly dysentery. Later, when the Nazis wanted bodies for their boxcars, people in the internment camps tended to be first on the list. Dave, I want to know more. I want to see where this took place."

Dave nods. I can tell he is thinking. "André!"

The silent man appears at our table. In a low voice Dave asks, "André, Nate here would like to see Les Milles. It's somewhere north of Marseille. Do you know how I can find it?"

André's eyes cloud over. He is quiet for a while. "Camp des Milles - in Les Milles, part of Aix-en-Provence. This place, we are not proud of."

I can tell this is a sensitive subject for him. "I understand, André. I have read about this place and the people who helped the Jews. I would like to visit." I wait patiently as André thinks. He nods and walks into the café. "I hope I didn't upset him."

"No, he's just thinking. Believe me, if you had upset him, you would know. Wendy and I only made that mistake once." Dave returns to his meditative gossip state as I contemplate what I have learned about the Jews of southern France during the war years.

When the Germans occupied northern France as part of the peace agreement, no one knew what to expect. For Jews all over France, it meant registering as Juif. At first, that simply involved a stamp on their papers. Eventually, in the Occupied Zone, it meant wearing a star. Some Jews followed the new laws, while others avoided them altogether. And then there were those who wore their Stars of David when it was convenient and took them off when it wasn't—mainly young people trying to avoid curfew, and of course, the resistance.

Shaking my head, I think about how hard it must have been to live in those times. Here in Provence, the Vichy government was in charge. But they weren't much better than the Nazis. They readily rounded up anyone the Nazis asked for. The Vichy may have officially controlled the Free Zone, but daily life was shaped mainly by local officials. So, when quotas needed to be filled, some towns tried to avoid their neighbors and chose non-French nationals.

I wonder if there were any Jews here in L'Esprit du Rhône. Were any of them rounded up? Did any of them try to escape? Looking around me, I find it hard to believe that the people of this quiet town would willingly send their fellow Frenchmen to die.

André returns and hands Dave a piece of paper. "This place is soon to be memorial. Not all French wanted innocents to die. This place tells their story." André's eyes cloud over, and he seems to be in a different time.

"Thank you, André." I nod in gratitude as the silent man lumbers away.

"Dang! I don't know what you stepped in, but I've never seen André like that."

"I get the feeling I opened the door to some old memories; a door he'd rather not look behind again."

"Looks like we have our mission for the day." Dave waves the paper at me. "Let's head back to the villa and let the others know where we'll be today."

The freeways in southern France are wide, easily accessible, and on this day, hot and sunny. After an hour and a half of high-speed travel, we drop off into the cool, quiet village of Les Milles, a small enclave outside Aix-en-Provence. Winding through the peaceful streets, we find our way to the camp outside of town, aptly situated on the "other side of the tracks."

Les Milles was once a tile factory before it was converted into an internment camp. The reddish-brown brick building is located across the street from the parking lot. The area is bustling with people raking the grounds, setting up stands, and preparing for what we later learn will be the inauguration ceremony in September.

Probably because many people are coming and going as they work to meet the deadline, no one stops to ask who we are or what we're doing there. We find our way into the building and quickly become captivated by the story the displays tell. The old factory, originally built to produce tile, became home to some of the greatest minds of the 1930s, including artists, historians, writers, and scientists. Even a Nobel Laureate spent time here. These Jews, trying to escape Nazi persecution, fled Germany before the war started, only to end up in a place that would later send its residents to Dachau and Auschwitz. Thanks to Varian Fry, an American journalist, two thousand Jewish intellectuals and artists were able to escape that fate.

Along with the American escape route, many others from around the world did their best to ensure refugees avoided death. The memorial shares the stories of the Righteous Among the Nations, individuals who risked their lives to save Jewish people. Many of those honored in the memorial were French men and women who protected the persecuted. These were people who valued liberté, égalité, fraternité. They valued these principles so highly that they were willing to face the consequences. Many paid that price, but their selfless efforts saved many more lives. These are the French men and women whose stories have not been told enough.

My heart aches and swells at the same time—the pain of horrific loss and the goodness of mankind. Together, they create a feeling I've never experienced before. This story needs to be told. We must teach not only the horrors of war but also the beauty of the human spirit and our connection to one another.

Dave must feel the same, as we have no words for each other. Somberly, we return to the car and head to Bonne Vie, each of us lost in our own thoughts. When we get back, all I can manage is a muted "thank you" before I go to Lee's hammock to process everything I've learned.

Later in the afternoon, Lee finds me with an invitation to the pre-dinner gathering. After hours of drifting through thoughts about my life, my work, and the state of the world, I am ready to join the others.

The usually lively group is seated on the back terrace, talking quietly. When I arrive, everyone falls silent. I'm sure Dave has shared our story with them. Picking up a cocktail glass, I propose a toast.

"Here's to Les Milles, the memorial. Here's to the Righteous Among the Nations. And here's to change. May we understand the past and choose to create a different future." After a toast with our glasses, there are a few "amens", a "here, here", and a "yes" before the group returns to silence.

Dave speaks up. "You know, Pomme and André lived through that time. I wonder what stories they have to tell. We only ever seem to talk about the weather, vegetables, and wine."

"I don't get the impression André is interested in discussing those years. Remember how he reacted when you asked for directions to Les Milles? You might want to leave that door closed. But you know,

I can share what we learned today. In my years of teaching history, I've focused on numbers, dates, costs, and the size of armies on a battlefield, as well as the length of the front lines, but I rarely discuss the spirit of the people. The connections between people, regardless of which side they are on. Besides the story of the informal Christmas truce during World War I, when soldiers from both sides sang hymns together, we don't usually discuss people beyond their roles as soldiers. We need to focus on ordinary people—how they were connected and how they cared for each other. Maybe then we can avoid sending our young men to kill each other."

Josh clears his throat. "Becoming part of this community has made a difference in our lives." He looks at each of his friends. "We are Americans, yes. Our French is not the best, and the way things are done here seems odd to us, but we and the people of L'Esprit du Rhône have learned to appreciate each other and want the best for one another. Nate, if you can get university students to understand that different doesn't mean bad or wrong and that we accomplish more through love than fear, you will have done something major."

Everyone raises their glasses again, "here, here."

"Now to write a proposal for the dean. I had so many ideas come to me this afternoon. I need to get them on paper. I'm looking forward to this!"

Wendy chimes in, "Sounds like you now have something to do and someone to do it with."

I laugh. "You've been listening. No more whining for me." I look skyward. "Andrea, you were right. I do still have something to do with my life. Thanks for the push in the backside."

Everyone laughs as we down our cocktails, and a lightness returns to our group as the magic of this place unites us.

15

Foreigners

ADRIEN & JÁNOS, NOVEMBER 2012

"THANKSGIVING? "Qu'est-ce que c'est?"

"It is an American holiday. The Americans celebrate this holiday by eating turkey and other American foods. Remember last year, they were looking for **cranberries**? Josh."

I can see that Celest doesn't know who I am talking about.

"The man with the smile." A look of understanding passes her face. "Made a sauce with **grosseilles** because he couldn't find cranberries. This year, he says a friend brought **cranberries** in a can."

"So that huge **dinde** you have hanging is for the villa?" Celeste points to the giant bird behind me.

"Oui, they ordered it at the start of the month. They insisted it be at least 7 kilos. I had to call Jacques in Orange to find a bird that big. And of course, the head and feet must be removed before it's delivered to the villa. Seems Americans don't like looking at a bird that is looking back at them.

"Ah, those strange Americans. When will they learn to be French?"

"They are trying. Last week, Wendy came in to ask how to make cassoulet. She doesn't like to ask the smiley man for advice. I think they are having problems in the kitchen."

"Better in the kitchen than the bedroom."

"No, the smiley one is married to the man who thinks he is French. The woman is married to the man who eats croissants at André's every morning."

"Oui, oui. He is there every morning, listening. Maybe one day he will learn to speak French. These foreigners can be so strange."

I smile and nod as Celeste leaves.

Foreigner. What makes someone a foreigner? Is one foreign if one does not speak the language? Or is it that someone doesn't know the way things are done? Or is one foreign if one's parents were not born in this country? If that is the case, then I am half foreign. Papa wasn't born in France.

The worst part is that I didn't know Papa wasn't born in France until **grand-père** Roger passed away. I knew Papa was adopted, but I thought he was one of those children whose parents died in the war. I believed **grand-père** and **grand-mère** took him in when he was a baby. I had no idea Papa wasn't French. A child never thinks to ask his father if he is a foreigner. Before that day, Papa said nothing about his life outside of L'Esprit du Rhône.

I remember the day I learned who Papa was. We had buried **grand-père** and returned to the house where neighbors had prepared a meal. It seemed the entire town had come to say goodbye. Everyone knew **grand-père** Roger. He had been L'Esprit du Rhône's butcher for almost fifty years. Even after Papa took over, grand-père still spent time behind the counter helping his neighbors. **He** was happiest when he was holding court in his butcher shop.

At the house, tables were set up in the yard, and people clustered together, reminiscing. I was 15, and it was my job to refill wine glasses that were running low, so I found myself moving in and out of conversations.

Roger was a lucky old coot having János come into his life.

WE were lucky that János came into Roger's life.

Yes, I remember the sour puss Roger had become after the war.

What do you expect of a man who lost his only son to a war with an enemy that became our allies and eventually our oppressors?

To lose a son the day before the Armistice, though. That was a real blow.

So sad for Roger.

"Who is János?" I thought. "Did **grand-père** and **grand-mère** have another son?"

Poor Jean, losing a father again.

Losing a father to the grim reaper of old age is nothing compared to having your family killed by a band of communists.

Not all communists are evil.

Only because your father worked with the Résistance do I accept those words.

János? Gaston? Communists? My father's name is Jean, and my mother's name is Julia. These pieces of conversation didn't fit the story I knew. My mind was whirling as I continued to pick up snippets of the past.

At least Sophie has a son to care for her now.

Her spirit almost disappeared when Gaston died at the Maginot Line.

Who would have thought she would get another son?

A son who gave her grandchildren and made her a **grand-mère**.

So grand-père and grand-mère did have another son.

Julia chose a good man.

Yes, János turned into quite an honorable Frenchman.

A good woman can do that for a man.

By the time the evening was over, I was confused and a little scared. After the well-wishers had left us with an empty silence, I approached Papa. "Papa, who is János?"

It was as though he'd turned to stone. He stopped breathing, and the blood drained from his face. Fear filled my heart. Who was this János to cause such a reaction in Papa?

After a long time, Papa took a deep breath. His body sank. His shoulders turned forward, and his eyes cast downward. "János was someone I knew a long time ago. Someone I tried to leave behind." Papa rubbed his eyes as if to clear his memory. "A scared boy who scratched his way out of hunger and cold to become a man with a life that no one could take from him."

"Why does he scare you, Papa?"

Shaking his head wearily, he sighed. "He is not what scares me. What scares me is the memory of being him. The memories of sadness, hunger, and the fear of being alone." He shook his head. "But I wasn't alone. Dominik saw to that, and when we had to part ways, he left me with hope."

"Papa, who was Dominik, and why were you cold and hungry? I am so confused. **Papi and Mamie** loved you. "

"The story is old and will take a while to tell. It is probably best that your sister and your mother join us."

Maman knew that Papa was not born in France and that Roger and Sophie had adopted him. But she had never heard the whole story. From the few details Papa had shared, she understood those memories caused him great pain. Maman loved Papa too much to pressure him to talk about them. It had been a long day, but none of us could sleep until we heard Papa's story.

I was born János Tóth in Budapest, Hungary, before the war began. My family, **Mère**, Léna, **Papa**, Élek, and *soeur,* Zóe, and I lived outside the city. My father was a carpenter, and we lived comfortably - we had enough food and a roof over our heads. Papa was a pragmatic man. He didn't see the point of taking sides when it came to who ran the country. All he wanted was to work and provide for his family.

In 1944, when the Nazis arrived, there was little construction going on; people repaired what they had, sometimes asking Papa to do the work. When the opportunity came for Papa to earn a little extra, he was grateful. The Nazi general who ran the nearby garrison wanted a sunroom for his wife, and he asked Papa to build it. Papa did the work to support the family. As he said, "One day the Germans will be gone, and we will still be here."

He was right. After the Nazis were defeated, Hungary began the process of governing itself once again. Many parties struggled for power, but ultimately, it was the communists who took control under the Soviet forces, who were "overseeing" the rebuilding of the country after the war.

In 1949, when I was 14, the communists decided I should join the party's farm program, so on a cold spring morning, I marched out of Budapest with other young patriots who were being ***retrained to feed the country***. Maman cried while Papa shook his head in concern for me and our country. I wore a stern expression and did my best to focus on my duty. What none of us knew was that it would be the last time we would see each other.

Six months later, one of the neighbors called Papa a fascist. The neighbor, Geza, envied my Papa. Life was not going well for Geza. He had no friends and no job. His anger at the world boiled over everywhere he went. The work Papa did for the German general had been a job, nothing more. But now, with the communists fighting for power, Geza saw Papa's past work as a chance for revenge. He twisted the story of Papa's work for the German general to fit his narrative, and he shared it with anyone who would listen. According to Geza, Papa was a Nazi, supported the fascist party, and was trying to undermine Hungary's move to communism. Someone needed to do something about Papa and his fascist ways. One October morning, members of the local communist party arrived at our house to do just that. They gathered the entire family and shot them. It was a message to the community—fascism would not be tolerated.

The tragic news reached me through a comrade at the farm. His mother had sent him a letter warning him to stay away from me and my "fascist ways." I was heartbroken and confused. Papa would never take sides in politics. My family's deaths were pointless. Between the pain and confusion, I found myself slogging through the day, barely able to complete my chores and little else.

It was Dominik who urged me to leave the farm and escape the Communist Party. He had seen what fear could do to a community. A neighbor family in his town had run away after local Communist Party officials harassed them because a relative in another city had supported a non-Communist candidate in the election. Life became so difficult that Dominik's neighbors had fled in the middle of the night. Their home and possessions were divided up between the people in the town who professed to be "good communists." With my family being marked as Nazis, it was only a matter of time before word made it through the communist party's hierarchy, and I too, would be shot as a fascist. Sadly, I didn't care enough to think about the consequences, much less find a way to avoid them.

It was Dominik who decided we should make our way to Austria. If we went together, we had a better chance of surviving. Bewildered and uncertain, I let Dominik guide me. We gathered scraps of food and headed into the woods, avoiding roads and anyone connected to the party.

One evening, a few weeks after leaving the farm, the smell of roasting bacon drew us to a campfire. As we crept closer, we saw a group of boys about our age. Our better judgment told us, "Keep to yourselves," but our stomachs answered the call of the roasting pork. Thinking we were on our way to a new farm assignment, like them, the group invited us to join them. That night, we ate bacon, drank palinka, and shared stories about life on the farm and how the communist party would ensure that all Hungarians received their fair share of the country's bounty. Near dawn, Dominik and I wandered into the woods to relieve ourselves. After a brief discussion, we agreed it was best to leave before anyone could figure out our true story.

We survived the following weeks by sleeping in barns, haystacks, and abandoned buildings. We ate potatoes left in the fields from the harvest. We foraged for mushrooms and secretly milked cows, and when we could, we worked for room and board. By the time we reached the Austrian border, we were exhausted and clothed in rags.

Cautiously, we approached the clearing marking the border between Hungary and Austria. Everything seemed peaceful, but not knowing how the border was patrolled, we decided to wait until the sun set. As daylight faded, the hollow howls of dogs tracking a scent drifted towards us. Months of built-up fear overwhelmed us.

It was Dominik who decided we should part ways. To this day, I can feel the cold and hunger I experienced that night, but mostly, it's the fear that haunts me. Dominik's words are burned into my memory. "They cannot follow both of our scents. We will meet in Vienna. Sunday on the steps of the City Hall. Be there! I will be waiting." And then he was gone. That was the last thing Dominik said to me.

Fear-fueled adrenaline powered my legs as I ran across the field and into the woods. I ran until I reached a road. I hoped I had run far enough, but I wasn't certain. After months of avoiding roads, I followed this new path from the safety of the woods. With heavy steps, I trudged among the trees for what felt like hours until I came upon a sign. In the dark, I struggled to make out the German letters.

Wien 88km.

I was in Austria! I had made it! I dropped to my knees in gratitude. Rolling onto my back, I lay crying as the stress of months on the run left my body. Somewhere during the night, I slept, with howling dogs and men with guns stalking my dreams. Waking to winter sunlight filtering through the bare branches of the trees above me, the memory of having reached safety came to me. I didn't have to hide. No one in Austria was looking for me. No one would send me back to the farm, or worse, put me before a firing squad.

As I realized I no longer had to hide, I shifted my focus to where I was headed. I had a clear mission: to meet Dominik on the stairs of Vienna's City Hall. Each step took me closer to reuniting with Dominik. We would dance to celebrate our freedom. We would toast with Vienna's famous hot chocolate. Together, we would find jobs and a place to live and rejoice at being alive. This dream pulled me forward.

Later in the day, the driver in a passing truck slowed for a curve and glanced my way. I must have caught his eye, as I had been dancing with joy at planning my reunion with Dominik. I gave the driver a sheepish smile and nodded.

"Where are you headed, son?"

"Vienna."

"I'm headed to Himberg outside of the city. I can take you that far."

Giving me a closer look, he hiked a thumb toward the back of the truck filled with bags of potatoes. "You can ride out back."

After months of walking, a ride—whether inside the cab or not—felt like a gift. I jostled among the bags, reflecting on the other gifts God had sent me. Naturally, Dominik was at the top of that list, but I also thought it was fortunate that I had learned some German from the soldiers garrisoned around us in Budapest. I wasn't fluent, but I could get by with simple sentences—something I would need in Vienna. When a potato rolled my way, I took it as another gift. Saying a prayer of thanks, I enjoyed each crunchy bite.

The truck pulled up in front of a small house, where my benefactor began unloading the bags. It seemed only right that I pitch in. After dropping the last bag in the cellar, I found the woman of the house waiting for me.

"You look like you could use some food. We don't have much these days, but we can spare an extra plate," she said, stepping back to study me. "I'll bring you some water to wash up before you come in."

Dunking my filthy hands into the steamy pan of water, I worked up a lather washing my face, neck, and arms, not only cleaning the grime of months on the run but releasing the struggle of the past few months as well. Tossing the water to the ground, I carried the wash basin into a house filled with the scent of cooking. My stomach began to quiver, and my mouth to water. Surely, sharing this humble meal would be the best gift of the day.

From my hosts, I learned that many Hungarian refugees had been on the roads since the Communist Party took control of Hungary. Organizations had formed to help those of us fleeing our country; in fact, the local Catholic Church was aiding refugees. My host recommended I speak with Father Eder. Thankful to the family for their hospitality, I headed to the church. There, I had my first bath in months and received a new set of clothes. Sleeping under a roof in a room full of other boys felt unsettling at first, but my stomach, satisfied after a meal, prompted the rest of my body to relax and finally fall asleep.

During breakfast, the other refugees shared cheerful conversations about their futures. Some were headed to Switzerland, while others were bound for Sweden. Two sisters chatted about their trip to America, where they would stay with an uncle. Everyone wanted to know which country I wanted to live in. I had only one focus: finding my way to the steps of Vienna's City Hall to keep my promise to Dominik. Rested and fed, I wished everyone luck with their new lives and headed to Caritas Austria in Vienna.

On Sunday, I woke up early, eager to reunite with Dominik. I couldn't wait to tell him about my journey and learn about his. Watching the sunrise and the light spread across Rathauspark, I dreamed of where we might go. To me, it felt like the whole world was open to us, and with Dominik, I was sure life would be good. The day passed slowly, and my excitement began to fade. Maybe Dominik had had to walk to Vienna. He might not have trusted anyone to give him a ride. Dominik would be there next Sunday, and I would be waiting for him.

To pass the time and earn some cash, I took on odd jobs. I carried packages for busy women leaving the market and swept stairs and sidewalks. One day, I lucked upon a perfectly good newspaper that I was able to sell to a man rushing for the streetcar. The following Sunday, I went back to the steps of City Hall. I was sure Dominik would be there. Once again, Dominik did not appear. Thinking of Dominik and how he had saved me, I promised myself I would be a patient friend. I would come to these steps for as many Sundays as it took.

Some Sundays, as I sat on the building's steps, the demons of guilt would attack me. Did I make it to Austria because Dominik led the dogs and soldiers away from me? Did I survive because he didn't? I had already lost my family. Losing Dominik felt impossible. I couldn't bear the thought that I might be to blame for his death. On the days that guilt consumed me, I had to remember that my family and Dominik would want me to move forward and be happy. Until I knew otherwise, I would not give up hope of seeing Dominik again.

Weeks went by, and life settled into a routine. On Mondays, I shined shoes for men who wanted to start their week off on the right foot. On Tuesdays, Ms. Hofer paid me to accompany her to the market. On Wednesdays and Thursdays, I stopped at stores to look for packages to deliver. On Fridays, I shined shoes for men heading to the opera. Then, on Saturdays, I helped at the church to prepare for Sunday services. When it was slow, I used some of my earnings to buy newspapers and sold them to men waiting for the streetcar. It was on one of those days that life changed forever.

The morning rush had eased, and I was left with a newspaper. Shrugging, I tucked the paper under my arm and headed back to the church to assist Brother Bauer with a project. After a few blocks, a well-dressed man asked if the newspaper was for sale. "Of course!"

As I handed him the paper, our eyes met. There was a light in his eyes and a smile on his lips. A warmth of welcome and belonging radiated from this man. It was a feeling I hadn't experienced since leaving home. The next morning, I bought a newspaper and hurried to the same street, hoping to see him again. I didn't have to wait long. Seeing me, he reached into his pocket for change and thanked me for the paper. After that, our morning exchange became an enjoyable part of my daily routine. Except on Sunday, of course, when I went straight to Rathausplatz and City Hall to wait for Dominik.

On Monday, the man seemed relieved to see me.

"I was afraid you had abandoned me."

"Oh no, Sir. I have an appointment at City Hall on Sundays."

"I was unaware the city did business on Sundays."

"No, Sir, I do not go into City Hall, I wait on the steps for my friend."

"How do you and your friend spend your Sundays?"

"Oh, how I would like to tell you about our day together, but he has yet to appear."

"What kind of friend is that?"

"Oh, an excellent one, sir. Were it not for him, I would not be here, and most likely not even be alive."

Something about this gentleman prompted me to share my story. His patient eyes and nodding head indicated his willingness to listen. As I neared the end of my tale, I realized the man probably had other matters to attend to. "I am sorry, sir, but I have taken too much of your time."

"What is your name, son?"

"János Toth, Sir."

"And your friend's?"

"Dominik Biro."

"My name is Louis De La Cour. Pleased to make your acquaintance. Now, can I depend on you to have my newspaper for me each morning, Monday through Saturday?"

"Yes, sir!"

The man handed me a 50-shilling note and told me to keep the change.

"Until tomorrow, Sir!"

On Saturday, M. De La Cour invited me for a cup of hot chocolate. Hot chocolate was a treat I had been saving to share with Dominik. But I felt it was wrong to decline M. De La Cour's invitation.

During our meal, M. De La Cour told me that his contacts in the refugee community had located Dominik. My heart fluttered with hope. The good news was that Dominik had made it to Austria. The rest of the news was bittersweet. Dominik had been injured during his border crossing and was found by the Red Cross, which took him to a hospital in Wiener Neustadt. By the time he was strong enough to leave the hospital, plans had been made to send him to England, and that's where he was now. M. De La Cour mentioned he would be glad to see that a message reached Dominik if I wanted to write to him.

I was glad to hear that Dominik was doing well, but he was so far away. I had been dreaming of our reunion and felt a great sense of disappointment. I had such dreams for us. As I thought about our journey from the farm to the border, I realized how fortunate we had been to share that path; now, it seemed Dominik had a new journey ahead. I would write to him and wish him a good life. In the meantime, I needed to find a new direction for mine.

I thanked M. De La Cour for sharing the good news and told him I would have a letter for him to post on Monday. Since I no longer needed to wait for Dominik on Sundays, I could bring M. De La Cour his paper every day.

M. De La Cour smiled with an understanding look. "How would you like to work for me? I need a messenger who knows the city and whom I can trust. The job will require you to interact with wealthy and influential people. These are businessmen and philanthropists who want to create a new Europe. Do you think you can move among such people?"

I had spent a month observing the businessmen of Vienna. I knew how they dressed, how they carried themselves, and how they spoke. I knew when to offer a full shine or just a quick buff. I knew when a man was too lost in thought to approach and when he had change to spare. As I listened to the men talking, I could tell which ones were truly friends and which were just being polite. "Yes, I can do that." As I smiled at M. De La Cour, I knew this was the new direction I was seeking.

Monday morning, M. De La Cour took me for a haircut and a new set of clothes, explaining that an appropriately dressed messenger would find more open doors than one who was less well-groomed.

Tuesday, when I met M. De La Cour, I was dressed for my new job. My assignments took me to concierge desks in nice hotels and a few government offices. While I waited, I listened carefully and watched who came and went. Over time, I discovered that M. De La Cour was a banker whose employer, Monsieur Chalon-Arlay, had sent him to Vienna to coordinate funding for various charity organizations. International groups had gathered in Vienna to attend a convention on refugees. The delegates at the convention defined who was a refugee, the rights of refugees, and the assistance they could receive. Working for M. De La Cour made me feel good, as if I were repaying the debt I owed for the help I had received.

By the time M. De La Cour finished his work, I had been inside the City Hall building, whose steps I had sat on for so many Sundays, as well as numerous other government offices and embassies. And, over those months, M. De La Cour had purchased two more sets of clothing for me. Being sixteen years old and eating regular meals, I had experienced quite a bit of growth. The summer of 1951 would turn out to be a season of significant change for me in many ways.

At the end of August, M. De La Cour and I met at the same café where we had met in the spring. M. De La Cour thought we should end my employment arrangement where it had started.

"You're a bright young man, János. How long has it been since you were in school? "

"School, sir? Hmm, when the communists took over, they figured I'd had enough schooling. After all, I could read, write, and do math. What more did a farmer need?"

"Is there anything you would like to study? You don't strike me as a farmer."

"You are right, I am no farmer, but I am not in a position to attend school. Now that you're leaving Vienna, I'll need to find a new job. And I'm pretty sure the church would like to see me move on. Brother Bauer will be sorry to lose my help, but I'm sure they would like to give my bed to a new refugee."

"How would you like to come back to France with me? You could stay with my staff, attend school, and do odd jobs at the bank. You will need to learn proper French, but based on what you've learned this summer, I don't think that will be a problem. You're an excellent observer of people and a quick learner."

"I am 16, sir. An age when most boys are looking for jobs."

"I understand, but with my support, you can take a few years to finish your education. This is something I would like to do for you."

Having no job lined up and having found M. De La Cour to be a man of his word, I accepted the offer. Dominik was building a new life in England; I could create mine in France. The next day, I thanked Brother Bauer and the church staff, packed my belongings, and met M. De La Cour at the train station.

Returning to school after two years and in a new language was challenging. I was older than my classmates and didn't fit in. However, I enjoyed my work around the bank and at the De La Cour estate. But my favorite chore was when the cook sent me to pick up the meat she ordered from la boucherie. I especially liked it when there was a long line, as it gave me time to watch your grand-père. Back then, his personality was gruff, and he could be a bit rude. I didn't care because, through it all, I could see his love for his work. When he talked about cuts of meat and how to prepare them, a window to his soul seemed to open, and I could see the man inside. Watching grand-père and the workings of the butcher shop fascinated me.

Our rocky relationship changed one windy fall day. I arrived to find a long line, so I leaned against the wall to wait my turn. As customers came and went, the wind blew in bursts of leaves. As the leaves danced at my feet, I spotted a broom against the opposite wall. Between customers, I swept up the stray foliage. When the door opened again, I shewed the entire bunch out of the opening and stood guard against any newcomers.

Between customers, grand-père looked me up and down, glanced at the broom, and nodded. When my turn came, he handed me the cook's order and grunted, but from that day on, our relationship began to change. Grand-père started to tell me how the meats should be prepared and the best sauces to pair with them. When I was in the shop, he made sure I could see what he was doing. After a while, I began asking questions, and he would answer them. As our bond grew, Grand-père changed. He became friendlier to his customers, and he seemed to move with more ease.

At the end of that first school year, Grand-père asked if I would like to work at the butcher shop for the summer. I eagerly accepted, and M. De La Cour freed me from my chores at the bank. During those months, I cleaned the shop, unloaded carcasses from the delivery truck, and learned the proper technique for sharpening knives - you know how Grand-père was about his knives. He even allowed me to grind meat. Throughout that time, Grand-père and I were filling the holes in each other's hearts. I learned that Grand-père and Grand-mère had lost their only son, Gaston. He died on the Maginot Line the day before the armistice. This loss had caused Papi great pain, which had translated into his gruff attitude. As our relationship grew, he became less of a curmudgeon, and this change was noticed throughout the town.

When fall arrived, I didn't want to return to classes, but M. De La Cour insisted I finish my studies. He would continue to free me from my duties at the bank and at the house, allowing me to work at the butcher shop in my free time, but he was insistent that I complete my education. Ultimately, Grand-père's agreement that I complete my education prompted me to return. By the time I graduated, I had decided to become a boucher. I moved into a small room at the back of the shop and settled into life as a butcher's apprentice. Papi, Mamie, and I became a family.

Not long after I left M. De La Cour's house, your Maman joined the estate staff. Your Aunt Beatrice was the estate cook at the time, and M. De La Cour had agreed to let Maman learn how to manage an estate kitchen. One of Maman's first tasks was to retrieve the estate's orders from la ***boucherie***.

Papa paused his story and looked at Maman. Taking a deep breath, a wan smile spread across his face, and his shoulders relaxed. It was then that I noticed that his leg, which had been bouncing, had come to a stop. Maman reached out and squeezed his hand, tears slipping down her face. Nodding to each other, Papa resumed his story.

I was glad to assist the new girl with her tasks, explaining which cuts of meat she was picking up and even suggesting ways to prepare them, though I knew ***Tante*** Béatrice already had plans for her order.

Papa smiled warmly.

Over the next two years, our relationship developed, and I realized Maman was the woman I wanted to marry. But first, I needed a home to share with her. The room at the back of the butcher shop wouldn't suffice.

Papi doubted the shop could support two families and was hesitant to pay me more. But when Mamie heard about my plans to marry, she took action. Mamie pointed out that I had become the son they had lost. I loved the butcher shop like Papi did. And my marriage to your Maman could bring children to continue the family business.

Papa smiled at Sophie and me.

As much as Papi loved his shop and valued its future, it was the happiness in Mamie's eyes as she and Maman planned our wedding that truly moved the old man. Not only did he realize that the butcher shop had enough income to support us, but he also announced that he wanted to adopt me.

I felt happy that Grand-père and Grand-mère wanted to adopt me, but I worried whether it was possible. I had no birth certificate, nothing to prove who I was, and there was no family left in Hungary to contact. I decided that M. De La Cour would know what to do. When I told him about Papi's plan to adopt me, he was overjoyed. He assured me my adoption could take place. Since the war, Europe had been full of displaced people. My situation was not uncommon. M. De La Cour assured me that he and Monsieur would work together to see that the proper paperwork was completed. And they did. The adoption process was finished shortly before you were born, my son, Adrien Gaston Petit.

That was the day I officially became Jean. I'd been going by Jean since my first summer at the butcher shop because it was easier for customers. That same summer, I made a real effort to sound like Jean, not János. The boys at school had teased me about my accent, and I really wanted to fit in, so I copied the way people in L'Esprit du Rhône spoke. Turns out I'm pretty good at copying sounds.

You see, I have become Jean Petit and am very happy. I didn't mean to keep my past a secret. I just didn't want to think about being János—about being alone and scared. I am grateful to M. De La Cour for bringing me here. I could never forget Papi, and I will always love Mamie. But it is your mère that I owe an apology to.

Papa looked into Maman's eyes.

I should have told you the whole story, no matter how scared it made me feel.

As Papa and Maman looked at each other, it was Maman's loving smile that said it all. She loved him whether he was János or Jean.

Papa passed away two years ago, but we still celebrate his birthday each year with Hungarian goulash in recognition of the scared but courageous boy who escaped Hungary. M. De la Cour Sr. saw something in that boy and brought him to L'Esprit du Rhône, for which we are grateful. Maman still shares stories of the happy young man she met at the butcher shop so many years ago, and we are reminded of what the love of community can do for a foreigner in a strange land.

16

The Treasure

DANIEL, JUNE 2013

Daniel,

My father loved his numbers.

I was born with a love of nature.

You, my beloved grandson, have received joy for both.

You are at a crossroads in life, and I fear I will not be here when you need me most. Please know that you could never disappoint me. My only request is that you don't disappoint yourself. Listen to the voice of the curious boy within you—he knows the way. Honor your father but never abandon that little boy. Life is long, and you must travel your own path. Be happy with yourself, and everything else will fall into place.

My gift to you is a trip to L'Esprit du Rhône and time to discover your path.

Love,

Papi

I CAREFULLY PLACE PAPI'S LETTER BACK INTO THE TATTERED ENVELOPE I've carried since I received it at the reading of his will during my last semester at Penn State. His words remind me how well he understood me. We had talked many times about my search for direction. Papi always listened, nodded in understanding, and showed that he trusted me to find my way.

Conversations with Papi were different from Dad's lectures. Dad was sure my path should follow his into the world of investment. He could open doors for me. Yes, I would have to start at the bottom, but he assured me that promotions and opportunities for growth would come quickly. I wouldn't have to struggle like he did. I would be a shining star in the investment world.

I enjoyed tracking the numbers, spotting trends, and knowing when to invest or withdraw my funds. Thanks to Dad, I've become quite skilled at it. Instead of a car for my sixteenth birthday, Dad gave me $5,000 to invest. He had spent the past four years teaching me about investments while growing my college fund. Now it was my turn to grow my funds, and there was a built-in incentive. The $5,000 was my college spending money. If I wanted to party, dress well, live off campus, or drive a car, I would need to turn that $5,000 into much more. He and Mom would cover tuition and room and board in the dorms, but beyond that, I was on my own. By the time I headed off to Penn State, I had a solid nest egg, enough to live comfortably during college. But by then, the investment bug had bitten deep, so even though I had money, I rarely touched my investments.

A month ago, I graduated with a degree in finance and management and a minor in environmental science. Today, I am flying to France. I shuffle through the envelopes that make up my inheritance from Papi. I opened the first one in the lawyer's office. I look at the second envelope.

Open upon graduation.

In it, I found information for my trip to L'Esprit du Rhône. Papi wanted me to fly out of New York City, the place where he first saw the United States, from the crowded deck of the steamer he and his family had taken from Portugal. Papi was eleven years old when the family arrived in New York. By then, the boy who was born in Paris had traveled through France, to Spain, and on to Portugal, staying ahead of the Nazi threat. In 1946, he arrived in a country he wouldn't have to leave. His butterflies of excitement told him he was finally home. Papi felt strongly about his French roots but felt even more strongly about the country that adopted him.

According to my itinerary, once I arrive in Paris, I am supposed to take a train to Avignon, where Papi has arranged for someone to meet me. According to Papi, I should stay in Provence for at least two weeks. I plan to walk the fields, talk to people, see the sights, and learn the history. No computers and no business—just time to get in touch with my French roots. I'm not sure if this trip feels like a vacation or a homework assignment.

Shifting to the third envelope, I read.

Open on your last day at the villa.

Hmm…I wonder what he had in mind for the end of my trip. I could open it now, but that would ruin the scavenger hunt, and Papi spent a lot of time creating this for me. We knew he had been busy with a secret project for his last few months. He had sworn his nurse to secrecy, so none of us knew what he'd been up to. Papi was beating the odds his doctors had given him, and he was happy every time we visited. So, whatever his project was, we were delighted for him. Papi loved puzzles, and it looks like his final gift to me was a well-orchestrated mystery.

The trip from New York to L'Esprit du Rhône had been long and exhausting, but Josh was adamant that I not sleep until the sun goes down. I figure I might as well start my assignment—walking through the countryside. The early June sunshine warms my body, and I feel my shoulder blades melt down my back. I get the sense I've been here before. Somewhere in my mind, there is a memory of this place.

I hadn't realized it, but Papi's stories had become a part of my memory. When I was little, he would tell me about his childhood adventures. His stories were so vivid that today I feel like I am seeing through Papi's eyes. I imagine being him—playing in the woods, running across fields, and splashing at the edge of the Rhône. I see the sunflowers, smell the lavender, and feel the cool shade of the plane trees. I find a trail along the Rhône and amble beside its slow-moving water. Thoughts of exams, travel plans, and Papi's mystery fade away.

My mind expands, and my thoughts drift away. Birdsong, the scent of lavender, and dappled sunlight pass through the void in my mind as I float into another world. When I come back to the present, I'm sitting by the river tossing stones into the water recalling Papi's voice telling me how he came to this magical place.

In 1939, I was five years old, but I sensed something was wrong. My parents spoke in hushed tones and only smiled when they were reassuring me that everything was okay. They weren't the only ones who had changed, though. All of the adults seemed worried, like they were waiting for something to happen, but I didn't understand what. After a few months, I started hearing the word WAR, and some of my friends' fathers went away to fight the Germans. Even though I couldn't understand what was happening, that strange feeling in my stomach told me it wasn't good.

Then the WHAT happened. German soldiers marched into the city. Large trucks menaced the streets, and new flags were draped over the fronts of buildings. Each day, the world seemed sadder and scarier. My body told me things weren't right.

On a June day when I was six, Papa came home from work early. He told Maman to pack bags for a trip. I was excited about going on an adventure, but as the key turned in the lock, I had a feeling that things wouldn't be the same after this trip.

At the curb sat a dusty old car, a car that Papa's boss had lent him. Papa quickly packed the trunk with the suitcases, and I was crammed into the back seat between large baskets of food. Papa explained that if we were stopped, he would tell the soldiers we were headed to visit a sick family member on the outskirts of the city. I didn't need my gut to tell me this was a lie. There was a quiet tension in the car as we moved through the city, Papa focusing on the road, Maman praying, and I too afraid to ask questions.

In the morning, I woke up to find the car parked next to a cluster of trees with the sun overhead. We ate breakfast of bread and cheese before Papa turned onto a dirt road in a place I'd never been before. We traveled on back roads; Papa explained that we were avoiding checkpoints. We only stopped in towns when we needed to fill the gas tank. That evening, Maman insisted we stop before it got dark so she could prepare a proper place for us to sleep. At twilight, Papa found a flat spot off the road and allowed her to create a cozy nest for us.

The next day, we wandered through hilly areas full of trees. Having spent my young life in Paris, I had never seen so many trees before. I longed to walk among them and stand under their leafy umbrellas. But no amount of begging could get Papa to stop unless it was to answer the call of nature.

The next day, the hills grew larger, and the woods grew thicker. With every kilometer, my excitement increased, but Papa became more distressed. We didn't know where we were or if we were even going in the right direction. As we watched the sun set at the end of the third day, we guessed we were heading southeast, but were we moving south fast enough?

Thankfully, the next morning, the road led us to the Rhône River. Papa decided that the river was a good sign and began following its course downstream. He reasoned that we would eventually reach the coast and find our way to Marseille, which he now explained was where we would look for a ship to take us out of France.

Crossing the river in hopes of finding a gas station, we wandered between towns, passing fields of sunflowers, lavender, and grapes. I hung out the window in awe, wishing I had drunk more water at breakfast so I could ask Papa to stop. I was daydreaming of exploring the fields. I wanted to see the different leaves and find out what was growing beneath them. I was pulled from my reverie by a rattling engine, followed by the car surging forward, taking a chug backward, and finally, the engine sputtering as the car stopped entirely.

Maman was sure Papa had waited too long to find gas, but he insisted the indicator was above empty. With no answer to the problem on the dashboard, Papa climbed out of the car to look under the hood. I scrambled out behind him. Now, Papa was a good accountant, but he was no mechanic. He peered beneath the hood, shifted his weight from side to side, and scratched his head as he tried to make sense of what he was looking at. Maman understood that we would be there for a while and began rummaging through the food baskets to prepare lunch for us. I wandered into the field to watch the bees as they buzzed from flower to flower. In no time I became immersed in the world around me, as I followed the bees through the rows of fragrant plants, over the rise, and out of sight.

My six-year-old mind raced. I was too busy being part of nature to feel afraid. I walked in and out of different patches of land, over a stream, and into a copse of trees. There was so much to see, feel, and smell! The breeze rustled the leaves; the birds called to each other. I was enchanted.

I understand why Papi sent me here! These are the fields he explored as a boy. He sent me here to be … enchanted! These fields, the woods, and the river have touched me the way they touched Papi. He knew I would understand. I sit in silent reflection until my empty stomach signals that it's time for that amuse-bouche Josh offered me earlier.

Josh and I sit in the villa's garden, watching the water in the fountain. Sipping his aperitif, Josh watches me wolf down a plate of ham-wrapped melon. "These are wonderful! I can't believe the taste of the melon; the ham adds the perfect amount of saltiness." I shove another bite into my mouth. "I don't think I've ever had a melon like this."

"Unless you've been to Provence before, it's pretty certain you haven't."

"Papi used to tell me he could never find melons in America like the ones he ate when he was a kid in Provence. He said that the best melon he ever ate was one he picked straight from the field. I remember the look in his eyes when he shared that story. I knew he was reliving the experience—in his mind, he was standing in the middle of a field of melons with juice running down his chin."

"Why not try it yourself? This melon came from Pomme's garden just outside the wall. We can visit tomorrow after he makes his dawn melon rounds. Each morning, he walks the rows with Chien, deciding which melons are ready to pick. He pushes the ripe melons into the path for one of us to collect later."

"Sounds like something Papi would approve of!"

Still on East Coast time, my body isn't eager to get out of bed. But after the pre-dawn serenade and the sunlight flooding my room, I have little choice. I gulp down a cup of strong coffee before following Josh out the door.

Stepping into the field, I take a deep breath of the cool morning air. I exhale and my heart opens to the world around me. I recognize this feeling. It's the same one I felt when Papi and I stood atop Mount Marcy watching eagles ride the thermals. We didn't speak; we didn't need to. The connection was deeper than words could say. Looking at the field before me, I can feel Papi beside me again.

While Josh has gone to get the wheelbarrow, I watch bees examine the freshly opened flowers on the sunny side of the garden. Standing here, I feel the earth's energy seep into my body. The energy rises as imaginary roots extend from my feet deep into the soil. The music of the planet vibrates within me. Is this what Papi meant when he wanted me to explore my French roots?

Josh returns with the wheelbarrow and a knife to cut the vines. Together, we work our way down the rows; he cuts the vines, and I stack the melons in the cart. At the end of the second row, Josh straightens up. "Time for a break and a snack." Pointing to the mound of melons, "Take your pick."

I tap a few dusty orbs before finding the right one. My mouth waters in anticipation, and I am not disappointed. The juice from the yellow-orange flesh runs down my chin and hands, and I eagerly lick my lips, not wanting to miss a drop of the sweetness. This was worth getting out of bed for.

When the melon is finished, we wipe our hands on our pants and go back to our task. While we work, I tell Josh how Papi used to help the boy who worked in the melon fields. "Papi learned when melons were ready to be picked and helped care for the whole field, pulling weeds, watering, and making a compost pile once the harvest was over. It seems the kid knew what he was doing. Papi told me his name, but it wasn't a common name like Jérôme or Leo. I remember Papi said it was some kind of nickname."

We leave the loaded cart in the drive leading to the road. "Pomme used to sell his stuff in town, but now that he's in his eighties, he's happy to share his harvest with us, André at the café, and a few other friends. The rest of the fruit, the co-op sells for him."

Feeling fulfilled, we head back to the villa, reliving our breakfast and talking about Josh's plans for lunch.

"Here comes our benefactor! Tuesdays are Pomme's days to go into town. He picks up bread, maybe some meat and cheese, and catches up on the latest gossip with André. You'll have to join Dave for one of his French lessons this week. It's his way of staying up to date with what's happening in town."

The dog that has been happily weaving his way in and out of fields spots us and trots our way. "Chien, how is my favorite pup this morning?" Josh leans down to give the dog a scratch, but the pooch avoids Josh's hand and heads straight for me. After a thorough sniff, Chien props his feet on my thighs and stretches up for a scratch.

"Hey, boy! Do I check out OK?" Remembering my manners, I nod at the old man. "Bonjour."

"Bonjour Pomme, voici Daniel, l'un de nos invités.Il m'a aidé à charger les melons ce matin."

"Good morning, Pomme, this is Daniel, one of our guests. He helped me load the melons this morning."

"Son grand-père vivait à L'Esprit du Rhône quand iil était petit et l'aidait à cuellier des melons."

His grandfather lived in L'Esprit du Rhône when he was a boy and helped pick melons.

The old man looks me up and down, nods and responds,

"Oui, et il s'est perdu dans les bois."

Josh looks from me to Pomme and back. "He says the boy got lost in the woods, too."

"Papi? Yes! He did. That's how he met the boy with the garden. The boy found Papi when he wandered away from the broken-down car."

"You said the boy with the garden had a funny nickname. It didn't happen to mean apple. "

"Yeah, that was it. I knew it was something strange."

"Daniel, meet Pomme. Pomme means Apple in English."

Pomme and Josh are having an animated conversation. "Wow! I can't believe your grandfather lived in our villa during the war. His parents fled Paris and were headed for Marseille. Their car stopped just down the road, and Madame and Monsieur took them in."

"Yes, Papi said they lived in L'Esprit du Rhône for a year. One day, Great grandpa announced they were going on a trip to the beach. Papi said he could tell something was wrong. His stomach always seemed to know when things were off, and when he saw tears in his mother's eyes, he knew it was right."

Josh turned to talk to Pomme again. "I asked him why the family left L'Esprit du Rhône. He says the people of L'Esprit du Rhône liked the kid and his family. They thought they were Jewish but didn't care. The Monsieur was respected, and the community trusted him. If Monsieur let the family stay in the villa, they were good people. But there was one man in town who didn't like Monsieur. This man thought he could get revenge on Monsieur and at the same time, convince the Germans to buy more of his wine. He sent word to his German contacts that Jews were living in the villa, but when Monsieur heard about the plan, he made sure the family was gone before the Germans arrived. "

Hearing about Papi from Pomme gave me new eyes. From Pomme's stories, I came to see Papi as the curious boy he was. As my stay continued, I allowed the little boy in my mind grow into a young man making his way in a new country, becoming a father, and then the grandfather I knew him to be. Papi had always been a man of inner strength and calm. He was a hiker and a defender of the natural world. Being here in L'Esprit du Rhône helped me understand that the time he spent with Pomme kept Papi grounded. This grounding allowed him to connect with the earth; no matter where he was, he could find the rhythms of nature, and that is what gave him such strength and peace.

Today is my last day at Bonne Vie. I lie in bed as the world wakes up. A heavy weight in my stomach pins me to the mattress. To clear the clutter in my mind, I take a deep breath. Tomorrow, I'll return to the world—a world where I have to make a choice. Do I work at Dad's firm and fulfill his dreams, or have the difficult conversation and disappoint him? How do I tell him I don't want to work on Wall Street, but I'm unsure of what I do want instead? There has to be a YES in answer to the NO I feel so strongly. It's time to move forward, but my YES is still unclear.

Struggling, I roll over. As I fight to free myself from the sheets, I glance at the dresser where I see the third envelope of my inheritance leaning against the mirror. My heart skips a beat. Today's the day I get to read Papi's final words to me. What did he want me to know today? The heaviness inside me begins to turn into butterflies of anticipation. Tomorrow can wait; today still belongs to Papi.

Daniel,

By now, you have come to understand the magic of this place. You have felt a connection to the land and hopefully found the answers you were looking for.

My final gift to you is my jar of treasures. The day we left for the beach, my stomach told me we would not return. I begged Maman to allow me to take my jar, but she insisted I leave my treasures behind. As a seven-year-old, those items were my most precious possessions. Not many would understand, but you, my boy, will see their value.

In the root cellar, on the wall beneath the dining room, you will find a place where the wall turns back upon itself. If you are on your knees and reach around the abutment, you will find the space in which I hid my jar. Only Le Chat and I knew of this hiding place, and I was sure he would never reveal it.

Love,

Papi

Papi left me his treasures? This was never a scavenger hunt; this has been a treasure hunt all along. I stumble into my pants and T-shirt and head to the kitchen.

"Wendy, good you're up!"

Startled, Wendy takes in my disheveled appearance. "Everything OK?"

"Better than OK." I wave my hand with Papi's letter in it. "Papi left me a treasure, and it's in your root cellar."

"Treasure? Root cellar? I'm not sure we have one of those. But come on, we can check it out." Drying her hands, she turns toward the door on the back wall. A slightly musty smell and cool, humid air greet us as we descend the stairs. Walking past an old furnace, we enter a room lined with shelves. On the shelves are jars of tomatoes, apricots, green beans, and other produce. I turn slowly, taking in the room and contemplating.

"A root cellar is where you keep vegetables. Right? Which wall is under the dining room?" Wendy looks at me questioningly. I wave the paper at her and read, "In the root cellar, on the wall beneath the dining room."

"Oh, that's the wall the dining room fireplace sets on." She points to the side of the room where the lines of shelves are broken up by what looks like a brick pillar.

I drop to my knees and crawl closer, peering to one side and then the other. It's dark and I can't see through the shadows, so I reach out to feel along the brick, extending my hand until I feel where the bricks end. There's a space between the pillar and the outer wall of the basement. Stretching around the pillar, my hand feels something glass—a cylinder-shaped object. My heart flutters as I grasp the jar and pull it into the light.

"I've never noticed that," Wendy whispers. "Is that Papi's treasure?"

I settle back on the floor, holding the dusty jar before me. In the basement's dim light, I can't make out the contents. "Let's take it upstairs so we can see better." I bolt up the stairs two at a time. By the time Wendy joins me, I have placed the jar on the counter where the sunlight streams in, dustily illuminating the shapes inside. I take a deep breath, look at Wendy, and nod. Grabbing the jar, I slowly twist the lid. After more than sixty years, it opens surprisingly easily. I peer in through the opening and chuckle, then sigh. Carefully, I remove the first item, the remains of an azure butterfly. For the past two weeks, I've been enchanted by their fluttering in Pomme's garden. Gently, I place the fragile wings on the counter. Underneath, I see the remains of an eggshell—a beautiful coffee-and-cream-colored shell with brown speckles. I found one on a walk through a field last week and asked Lee to help me talk to Pomme about it. Pomme told me it was the shell of a ganga cata—the birds whose morning song is part of the dawn's symphony that begins our days.

Next, I gently lift out a perfectly formed snail shell. It is enormous! I've seen many snails over the past two weeks, but none could hold a candle to this leviathan. Then, there is a piece of wood. I hold it up to the light and turn it to examine all its sides. Wendy squeals, "A dove, it looks like a dove. Like the ones that visit the garden."

Lastly, a smooth, round rock, perfect for skipping across the water. I laugh as I remember Papi teaching me how to choose a stone with the correct shape to bounce across the lake.

Papi was right. This is a jar full of treasures; treasures he chose to share with me. Treasures that will remind me of my time in L'Esprit du Rhône and my moments with Papi. No price can be placed on my inheritance—the trip, the time at the villa, and this jar of memories that reminds me of my French roots and the man with whom I share them.

Dave dropped me at the train station in Avignon early this morning. Now I am settled in my seat, watching the countryside pass by. In a few hours, I will arrive at Charles de Gaulle and then catch a plane back to New York. I pull out my journal and begin a new page - MY YES.

I don't know what MY YES is, yet, but now I have some markers to help me find it.

MY YES

My why is nature and my connection to it.

I want to

- have time to connect to nature
- preserve nature
- help others find peace in nature

MY SKILLS

- Grow money
- Manage money
- Manage people

I can see that managing money is still my what. But now I understand my why. A traditional Wall Street job won't do. I need to manage money for a purpose, and that purpose is to protect and share nature.

I review my notes and feel a sense of contentment. Papi was right; I would find my answers given the time and space, and the magic of L'Esprit du Rhône.

17

The Legacy

LOUIS DE LA COUR III, JUNE 2013

FEW PEOPLE KNOW THE HISTORY OF THE SMALL BUT POWERFUL Bank of Chalon-Arlay, or the part the De La Cour Family has played in its story. The day my father died, the De La Cour mantle and that story passed to me. Today, on my sixtieth birthday, I reflect on the part I have played and wonder what Monsieur and Grand-père would think of it. Selling the villa to the Americans was not a popular decision, but after four years as an empty sentinel, the villa needed someone to care for it. The excited Americans felt like the right choice.

I was raised to do this job. My father saw that I stayed in L'Esprit du Rhône until I was sixteen years old, thereby rooting me in this small town and allowing the community to see me as one of their own. In addition, I was tutored in English and German and sent abroad for university. My first years in banking were spent in the United States, where I developed an international perspective. All the while, I knew L'Esprit du Rhône was home and the Bank of Chalon-Arlay my destiny.

I was called back to L'Esprit du Rhône to begin that life two years before Monsieur died. I was here to ensure that Madame was cared for. When she passed, it was my responsibility to carry on the legacy of this influential couple and the distinguished institution they had left behind—an institution of influence for good in the world.

The bank's story wasn't always one of justice and goodwill. Established in 1852 in the Burgundy region of France, the business was housed on an upscale street in Dijon. In 1928, when the young Chalon-Arlay heir took the reins of this financial institution, it was like other banks—run by and for the rich and powerful. William Arnoux Chalon-Arlay II had more than enough money to live the life he pleased. He felt someone with such abundance was obliged to help those who were less well-positioned, so he set out to do just that. Unfortunately, many of the investments he considered were frowned upon by the bank's hierarchy. After months of struggling to create the institution that he wanted to lead, William Arnoux realized the firm needed reorganization. But what he needed first was a bank director who shared his vision and one whom the staff would respect.

In 1928, my grand-père, Louis De La Cour, was a junior manager at Bank Chalon-Arlay. He was regularly tasked with accomplishing the hows of upper management's decisions. When William Arnoux began making his seemingly odd requests, it was Louis who made them happen, much to the chagrin of the bank director and board. One day, William Arnoux overheard the bank director castigating young De La Cour for following the owner's directive without his, the director's, approval. As the story goes, grand-père sat calmly, and when the manager was finished, informed him that he agreed with the bank's owner and was happy to see him using his money for the benefit of ordinary people. At that point, the director informed Louis that his services were no longer needed. He could pack up and leave immediately. Although concerned about how he would support his family, grand-père calmly gathered his coat and hat and left the bank.

That evening, William Arnoux appeared at grand-père's door. "I would be most obliged if you would meet me at the bank at 10 am tomorrow. I have a project I need your help with."

"It would be my pleasure, sir, but the bank no longer employs me."

"I understand, but please do me this favor."

"Of course, sir."

When grand-père arrived the next morning, he was escorted to the director's office. Nervously following the clerk, grand-père wondered what Monsieur Chalon-Arlay had in mind and the director's part in it. Entering the office, grand-père found William Arnoux sitting in a chair in front of an empty desk.

"Good morning, sir." Looking around and not finding the director, grand-père suggested, "I can wait outside until you have finished your business with the director."

"You are correct, I am here to see the bank's director. We have much to discuss."

Grand-père turned to leave.

"I'd rather have that discussion face-to-face than through the door, however. Please have a seat." William Arnoux pointed to the chair behind the desk.

"Sir?"

"If you will accept the position, I would like to employ you as the new director of the Bank Chalon-Arlay.

"Sir?"

"I believe you and I share a similar view on the use of wealth and power. Together, we can make a difference in the lives of many people. This is the project I need your help with. Will you join me?"

That was the beginning of the De La Cour family's service to, and friendship with, Monsieur William Arnoux Chalon-Arlay II.

1928 was not finished being an eventful year for the young William Arnoux. During the social season that year, Arnoux attended a round of social events in Paris, thereby keeping his word to his mother that he would make himself available to the "right type" of young ladies. This meant that he was to attend balls where he could be seen by the mothers of such young ladies. Those mothers could make arrangements for invitations to smaller soirées where he might spend time in conversation with such young ladies and be further evaluated by their mothers. This was the last year he would play this silly game. It bored him, and so did the young ladies.

Inheriting the bank had initially raised his value as a suitable beau, but that was before news of how he was managing the bank spread through the haute bourgeoisie. A mother looking for a wealthy match for her daughter would not waste time on a man who acted "frivolously" with his money. William Arnoux didn't expect much from his presence, but he had promised his mother he would attend.

On that fateful night, the tall, lanky Arnoux mechanically followed his mother's requirements of attendance. Smile and nod when spoken to. Circulate about the room. Drink something and, for God's sake, eat something. Standing before a wide table laden with food, he reviewed his choices. Cheese, foie gras, roast pigeon, fruit, nuts…

"Caviar always shows one's good taste. But then I prefer the unladylike slice of ham."

At Arnoux's left elbow stood a delicate girl of 18—a quiet beauty with a hint of mischief in her eyes. "Then we shall each have a piece of ham," he announced.

"That would be grand, but Maman would have my head. I must be content with this glass of punch. It is all I am allowed until this fête is complete. I couldn't possibly find my mouth filled with food, should a young man make a quip to which I must respond. And God forbid a piece of food become lodged between my teeth."

"Ah, you, too, have been provided a script for this event."

"I made a deal with Maman; I play her silly game for the season, and the rest of the year, she doesn't bother me with talk of marriage. If she can't marry me off within this window of time, I get another year of freedom."

"I understand. This is the final year I will tolerate Maman's direction. Papa died this spring, so I agreed to one last round for her sake. These days, I find work to be more engaging than these parlor games."

"By work, do you mean giving away your money?"

"I am not giving away my money. I am investing it, just not where others think I should."

"I think it is brave of you to follow a sense of duty."

A clearing of the throat drew their attention to a nervous young man who had appeared beside Arnoux. The young man bowed, and with a quivering voice, he spoke. "Mademoiselle, I would be delighted if you would join me for a dance."

"How kind of you to ask, but I'm afraid this gentleman has beaten you to it." Looking into Arnoux's eyes questioningly, she offered her hand. With a dip of his head and a glance at his anxious rival, Arnoux drew Mignonne to the dance floor.

After that night, Arnoux did not wait for Mignonne's mother to send an invitation. Within the week, he had invited Mignonne and her mother to join him for a walk in the Tuileries, followed by chocolate at Angelina. This allowed him time to arrange travel and lodging in Dijon for mother and daughter. Since he understood his value as a suitor was firmly based on his ownership of the bank, he would play his ace up front. The first night of their visit, Arnoux hosted a fine meal at the restaurant of a little-known but excellent chef. The following morning, he provided an in-depth tour of the bank, followed by tea in the bank's private dining room. It didn't take long for Duchesse Dubois to respond with an invitation to dine with the Duc and Duchesse at their city home in Paris.

By then, Mignonne's mother, Duchesse Dubois, had done her homework and knew William Arnoux's distant relationship to William V of the Netherlands, albeit illegitimate. Arnoux's great-grandfather had been the result of a lustful liaison between William V and a daughter of the house of Burgundy. Arrangements were made to support the boy while William V found himself exiled to England. This turn of events made the use of the surname Burgundy a better choice than Chalon-Arlay. The funds that William V left for the child's care were quietly invested. It wasn't until Arnoux's grandfather took charge of these funds that banking became part of the family business. By the time Arnoux's father came along, the family's wealth and power were well known, so the surname Burgundy was exchanged for the rightful title, Chalon-Arlay. This checkered history meant nothing to William Arnoux. He had no use for titles and had little interest in creating more wealth and power. But if that was what Mignonne's mother needed to agree to this marriage, he would gladly allow it.

Mignonne's mother, the Duchesse Dubois, had worried her daughter would never find a suitable husband. Mignonne was beautiful and drew beaus like moths to a flame, but few returned after learning the flame not only burned but had a tongue that cut like a knife. Besides, Madame Dubois was the second wife of the duke, and he was her second husband. Mignonne, from her first marriage, had spent most of her life on her grandparents' estate outside of Avignon and had little interest in the games played by the aristocracy. This successful man of royal blood made Madame Dubois' life much easier.

Mignonne accepted Arnoux's proposal on one condition: they would live in the Vaucluse near her childhood home. Arnoux gave his word, and the match was made. The following June, the couple wed in Avignon's Notre-Dame de Doms, a compromise with her mother—a formidable setting, yet one that would keep them away from the critical eye of the Parisian elite.

By then, Arnoux had identified L'Esprit du Rhône as the town in which he would establish his reorganized bank. This provided Mignonne a base from which to find a home. A banking associate in Avignon had supplied Arnoux with a list of "appropriate properties" for Mignonne to consider. For a month, she and her driver diligently visited each one—many were too ornate, some too rambling, and the others uninspiring. When Arnoux asked what it was she was looking for, she just sighed, "I will know when I find it." Other husbands may have been frustrated, but Arnoux trusted Mignonne. She would find the right place for them.

Mignonne awoke one morning, tired of searching for a place to call home. Today, she would surprise Arnoux with lunch and share his joy in the bank's progress. Dressed to impress her new husband and sitting next to a basket of Arnoux's favorite foods, Mignonne found herself ready to depart with time to spare. "Jérôme, we are a bit early for lunch. Let's enjoy the countryside this morning." Lazily crossing fields of sunflowers, taking in the parallel lines of grape arbors and watching various crops being harvested, Mignonne was impressed with the area's bounty. She thought about how none of the properties she had visited had been near L'Esprit du Rhône. It struck Mignonne that the houses on the list she'd been given were selected for status and the need to impress. Neither she nor Arnoux felt the need to impress anyone. What they needed was a home that welcomed people and allowed Arnoux to access the bank easily. They needed a home near L'Esprit du Rhône.

As Jérôme drove past the open gates of a maison, Mignonne felt a tug on her heart. Leaning towards the open window, Mignonne peered into the estate, wondering what it was that called to her. From the roof line peeking above the wall, she could see that the house was a good size and handsomely built. She wanted to see more. "Jérôme, it's time we head for the bank." A month later, Mignonne was walking the rooms of the maison with her designer, discussing the latest styles and how to match them to the life she and Arnoux would lead.

Arnoux had known the moment Mignonne arrived at the bank that she had found what she was looking for. After a brief investigation, he discovered that the house had been built in 1854 by a wealthy land-owner who, due to poor investments during the Long Depression of the late 1800s, had sold off large parcels of land to cover his debts. By 1929, the estate had been reduced to 30 hectares, and the remaining family members had little interest in continuing to farm it. So, when Arnoux made a generous offer for the house and remaining land, there was little need for negotiation.

While Mignonne worked with designers to update the house, Arnoux finished working with Grand-père to build a bank on the town square. A few years prior, a fire had taken a block of buildings, leaving behind stately exteriors facing the fountain, but a charred skeleton within. By early 1930, the interior of the bank had been rebuilt. The De La Cour family, with a handful of the original bank employees, became part of the L'Esprit du Rhône community. The stage was set for this new, smaller bank to begin its mission in earnest.

The 1930s began with Monsieur lending money to small vineyards and other small businesses, those too small for most banks to consider. When the Spanish Civil War broke out, Monsieur supported the Republicans and their battle for the people. Substantial cash donations made their way to organizations and small groups of people Monsieur trusted to help the poor of Spain.

As the Spanish War was brewing, a darkness was also emanating from Germany. Much of Monsieur's wealth was invested in German banks and businesses, producing sizable returns. But in his heart, Monsieur knew he could not be involved with the evil growing there. Together, Monsieur and Grand-père decided to explore investments in America, so Grand-père sailed to New York. During his visit, he established accounts with J.P. Morgan & Co., a decision that would later bode well for Monsieur's portfolio. In the years that followed, funds were quietly moved from Berlin to the new account in New York, where they were judiciously invested in American businesses as opportunities arose.

With the American account in place, transfers of funds from British and French investments were easily accomplished as necessary. Monsieur could feel the winds of war blowing, and he wasn't comfortable with the direction they were headed. Keeping only a working capital in both Britain and France, Monsieur secured the bulk of his investments across the ocean. There was a very short conversation about moving Bank Chalon-Arlay completely out of France, but neither Madame nor Monsieur could bear to desert the people of L'Esprit du Rhône or the country they loved. The bank would stay, and so would they.

No one escapes the ravages of war, but L'Esprit du Rhône was blessed with relative calm during the early 1940s. The Vichy, being the party of the bourgeoisie, respected Monsieur's aristocratic blood and did little to disturb him or his business. They trusted he would support the French upper-class standards the party sought to uphold. The town's people understood that Monsieur could have left the country, but he and Madame had chosen to remain. The community's respect for his decision made the couple silent symbols of endurance. With the people of L'Esprit du Rhône reflecting Monsieur's calm demeanor, and the Vichy staying out of day-to-day life in the town, much of the war's wrath skirted the area.

A few in the community, communists and resistance members, chafed at the thought of living under the umbrella of an aristocrat. What they didn't realize was the part Monsieur and his bank played in supporting La Résistance. Mario hadn't disappeared by accident. He left at the request of Monsieur. It was Mario who served as the bank's connection with La Résistance in France. Few were aware of the midnight visitors to the villa during those years and the cash wrapped in clothing that was carried away in knapsacks. Much of the funds remaining in Monsieur's London accounts found their way to De Gaulle and his resistance efforts in England. During those dark years, money flowed out of the bank with no financial return expected. The only return Monsieur wanted was the return of égalité, fraternité, and liberté.

Monsieur was generous with more than his money. He had always had a knack for matching problems to solutions, and for one family, Monsieur's support was personal. Louis, Sarah, and Daniel were divinely delivered to the villa's doorstep, their escape from Paris cut short due to car trouble. Because of shifting Vichy power in the south and shipping disruptions on the coast, Monsieur thought it best for the family to remain at the villa under the guise of staff, gardener, maid, and son. For the city-bred accountant, this new position was a stretch, but with a bit of help from Pomme, he eventually made a passable groundskeeper. The community came to accept the couple and their spirited son. Everyone except Lucas. Lucas, the square peg who never wanted to fit into the round hole of L'Esprit du Rhône. Lucas, the son of L'Esprit du Rhône's most beloved vintner. Lucas, the Frenchman, who was sure the Germans could see his superiority.

Lucas had plans. He was sure he and the Germans could come to an arrangement. He would help them in their quest to rid Europe of Jews, and they would see that his wines were served at the finest tables in Germany. All he needed was to get word to the right people. Thankfully, the eyes and ears of the resistance were deeply embedded in the workings of Vichy France, so before word could reach the Nazis, the news found its way to Monsieur at Bonne Vie.

On a bright summer morning, Louis and his family set off for the coast, ostensibly to retrieve a fish delivery from Monsieur's favorite fishing boat, with a short side trip to the beach for the boy. This trip was but the first step of a many-layered escape route. That summer day, the captain of the fishing boat delivered his cargo to a small coastal village in Spain. The boat's captain, who had purchased his vessel thanks to a loan from Bank Chalon-Arlay, had no qualms about transporting friends of his benefactor. When the family landed, they were met by former Republican guards who transported them to Portugal. Guides walked the haggard family over the mountains to a river where they boarded a barge bound for Lisbon. In Lisbon, a bookkeeping position awaited Louis in a business underwritten years earlier by the Bank Chalon-Arlay. When word came from Portugal that the delivery had arrived, Monsieur's thoughts returned to La Résistance and the work needed to finish the war.

What Monsieur didn't know was that Lisbon would not be the family's final home. After the war, Louis and his family made their way to New York, where the industrious accountant found a place in an international firm. Once the family was comfortably established, Louis decided it was time to appropriately thank Monsieur and Madame for saving their lives. The announcement of thanks arrived at Bonne Vie in the form of a workman from La Cornue. He was there to measure for a bespoke Le Château oven. You see, Louis had been the accountant for Albert Dupuy, owner of La Cornue. Albert was so happy to hear that his former bookkeeper had escaped that he personally arranged for one of his newest ovens to find its way to the villa's kitchen, where it stands today.

In May of 1945, while the rest of France was celebrating victory over the Nazis, Monsieur was thinking of the future. He knew what lay ahead for Europe was an extensive rebuilding challenge. If the people of Europe wanted to avoid a third war in the coming decades, what was built needed to be different from what had been. The people of Europe needed to heal the great wound left by years of fighting and work together to create opportunities for the whole of Europe.

In 1946, Monsieur traveled to London to join like-minded men who were ready to put the war behind them. The devastation laid out for them was greater than anyone could comprehend. As the Germans had retreated, they had destroyed roads, bridges, railways, crops, hospitals - anything that would support life. Returning to L'Esprit du Rhône, overwhelmed by Europe's deprivation, Monsieur, Madame, and Grand-père struggled with where to begin addressing the broken continent's needs. It was Madame who provided direction - reunite families. People find ways to solve their problems when they have someone to live for. And so, the focus of Bank Chalon-Arlay shifted to supporting refugees and reuniting families. Six years before the world would convene in Vienna to address the refugee situation, forces within the small Bank Chalon-Arlay began their task, organizing food, clothing, transportation, and lines of communication between displaced peoples across the world. The funds Monsieur had moved to America were ready to be tapped.

The bank's work with refugees took a personal turn for our family in 1946 when Grand-père met Janós in Vienna. Janós's work as a courier impressed Grand-père. He knew he couldn't abandon the bright teenager, so he asked him to come to L'Esprit du Rhône. The easy-going Janós quickly fit into the household, and with my father off at university, Janós received much of Grand-père's paternal direction. Though Janós had enjoyed his time around the bank, it was his work with Roger at the boucherie that captured his interest. Grand-père was sad to lose his ward but was happy for him and the place he had made for himself in the community. The day Roger and Sophie adopted Janós, Monsieur reminded grand-père of their meeting at the bank—the day grand-père became director of Bank Chalon-Arlay. Monsieur had been sure he'd made the right choice, and watching Janós, Roger, and Sophie become a family reminded him that he'd been right. Hiring Grand-père as director of the bank was the second-best choice of his life. Second, of course, to marrying Madame.

As Europe began to rebuild, Monsieur's finances shifted back to Europe. A core amount found its way to high-yield ventures, while the rest of it financed individuals ready to rebuild their lives. Among those businesses were many small wineries that, thanks to loans and, in some cases, direct investments, were able to replace machinery and equipment lost during the war. One of those investments went to Jules Gagne, who had a vignoble outside of Carpenteras. Thanks to Monsieur's partnership in the winery, the produce from Madame's postwar grape vines was turned into the finest wine never sold. True to his word, Monsieur never sold one bottle of wine from the grapes grown at the villa. Jules gratefully turned the villa's grapes into a house wine that became famous, though never available to the public. Friends and associates who were gifted bottles from the villa's cellar were sworn never to sell them. The wine was a labor of love, given in love, and was expected to be shared in love; no financial gain was to be made from it.

Sadly, Camille, like her father, has never tasted the joy of sharing wine made from the Earth's bounty. Earlier this year, Josh asked Pomme's advice on nurturing the vines at Bonne Vie so that they may be used to make wine. Not wanting to see that door of discord reopened, Pomme suggested Josh carry on with his jelly-making and forget about entering the wine arena.

When Madame died, the remaining bottles of her wine collection were moved to the basement of Bank Chalon-Arlay. It seemed only appropriate that Bonne Vie's greatest treasure join the rest of Monsieur's wealth. Unlike the funds the bank manages, this wealth could not be spent or used to earn money. It was decided that this special wine would be served once a year, at a celebration held on Monsieur's birthday. Those who have been a part of the bank's story, whether large or small, are invited to remember the man who made a difference in the world. Reflecting the humility of the man whose birth they are celebrating, attendees refrain from speaking about the celebration in public. As the years pass, the list of original attendees grows shorter, but the appreciation for Monsieur's sense of duty to his fellow man has not been lost.

There were no heirs to Monsieur's estate—Madame had been unable to have children, and Monsieur's sister had died, leaving no children. Not wanting the money to be claimed by a possible distant bloodline and wanting the bank to continue making a difference, Monsieur's money & investments were used to create a foundation; the Bonne Vie Foundation. My father and I spent many months working with Monsieur to discuss a vision for the foundation's work, culminating in guidelines for future expenses and investments.

The bank would continue to invest a core amount of the money in a manner that generates funds to support the foundation's work. That work is to invest in people and small businesses. The bank itself would remain in L'Esprit du Rhône and continue to serve the town and surrounding areas while also housing the foundation's headquarters. Decisions on core investments would remain the purview of the banking staff, directed by criteria left by Monsieur. Investments in people, small businesses, and civic projects would be reviewed by the foundation's board - banking staff, and a select group of individuals whose lives had been positively impacted by such investments. The first board consisted of my father, Monsieur's lawyer, and me from the banking side, while André, Fabien, and Gérard made up the "invested" portion of the board. All involved solemnly determine investments and loans as they know Monsieur would have.

As existing board members age, the Foundation prepares for the future. A De La Cour will remain at the helm of the Foundation as long as one of us is able. My son's interests have led him into a career in music. But his younger sister has chosen a path in business. She intends to carry the banner of equality, which places her in line to replace me as board chairperson. Thanks to the Foundation's involvement in a civic project in Lyon, a bright new bank manager, Phillp La Crosse, has joined our fold. Philip has moved to L'Esprit du Rhône to learn more about the Foundation and his role when I am no longer able to participate. And these days, André has begun to talk of passing his place on the board to Claude, who has acquired André's fine art of matching problems to solutions. As long as these new board members remain committed to the roots of our Foundation—to support those less well-positioned in life—the world will continue to have a quiet but influential champion for good. The magic of Bonne Vie will go on.

"The best and most beautiful things in the world cannot be seen or even touched— they must be felt with the heart."

—HELEN KELLER

Acknowledgements

MY THANKS BEGIN WITH THE MAN WHO HAS BELIEVED IN ME SINCE the day we sat on my apartment floor, lost in conversation as a party swirled around us. Mike has been my partner in adventure, dreams, and everyday life. Without him, this book would never have come to fruition. The story of Bonne Vie began with a game of "What if…?" after stumbling upon a villa for sale during our first vacation in France. From this game, Mike encouraged me to write a story about friends who retire to Provence to run a Bed & Breakfast and the life that flows from it. Little did Mike realize the years it would take to complete the book, and publish it, much less the time and effort required to share it with the world.

Thank you to my parents, who not only saw that I received an inspiring education through many different schools and the international life we lived as a family, but also for sharing their self-publishing lessons with me. I am especially grateful to my mother, who continues to be my cheerleader every step of the way.

And where would I be without the friends who patiently listened to my writing adventures for years?

Many thanks to my writing group, whose nudges kept the story moving in the right direction.

This second edition would not be what it is without the aid of my friend Luc, who found all my errors in French and made sure I corrected them.

And lastly, very special thanks to everyone who purchases this book and shares the spirit of Bonne Vie with the world.

Glossary

CHAPTER 1 — L'ENCHANTER

L'Enchanter — the Enchanter

Le Chat — the cat

CHAPTER 2 — SECOND ACT

Gîte — holiday rental accommodations

Laissez le monde derrière vous, ralentissez et profitez de la vie. — Leave the world behind, slow down and enjoy life.

***Bricolage* — DIY, in the US, it is a hardware store**

"Bonjour! Deux cafés, s'il vous plaît" — "Good Day! Two coffees, please."

la Poste — post office

Allez à la banque — Go to the bank

L'Esprit du Rhône — Spirit of the Rhône

Mairie — City Hall

Boulangerie — bread store

Boucherie — butcher shop

Bonjour, puis-je vous aider ? — Good day, may I help you ?

Parlez-vous anglais? — Do you speak English?

Joie de vivre — joy of life

Promesse de vente — promise of sale

Notaire — notary

Marché immobilier — real estate office

Vin de pays — (French: [vɛ̃ də pei]; 'country wine') was a French above the vin de table classification but below the appellation d'origine contrôlée (AOC) classification and the former vin délimité de qualité supérieure classification.

Maison — house

Chapter 3 — Affair with French Architecture

Garbure — is a hearty, thick, rustic French soup or stew originating from the Gascony region in the southwest of France traditionally based on cabbage and confit d'oie,[1] though the modern version is usually made with ham, cheese and stale bread.

Cassoulet — a rich stew that is amalgamation of haricot beans, sausage, pork, mutton and preserved goose, aromatically spiced with garlic and herbs

Chapter 4 — Vibrations of the Land

Chien — dog

Maman — mother

Papillon — butterfly

Chapter 5 — Love's Return

Le jardinier — the gardener

Oui — yes

Un peu de nourriture — a snack

La République — the Republic, another name for France

Liberté, Égalité & Fraternité — Liberty, Equality & Fraternity

Le Chat — the cat

CHAPTER — 6 MAISON ROCHE

Imbéciles — idiots

Rêves Perdus — Lost Dreams

Grand-père — grandfather

CHAPTER 7 — FRENCH LESSONS

Laissez-faire — let it happen

Maire — mayor

Bonjour, mon ami. Une tasse de café et un croissant, s'il vous plaît. L'addition, s'il vous plaît. Merci. Passez une bonne journée. — Good day, my friend. A cup of coffee and a croissant, please. The bill, please. Thank you. Have a good day.

Mistral — wind in southern France

Excusez-moi — Excuse me

Question du jour — topic of the day

CHAPTER 8 — THE HABANERA EFFECT

Mais si je t'aime, si je t'aime, prends garde à toi — translates to **"But if I love you, if I love you, be on your guard!"** This line is from the Habanera aria in Georges Bizet's opera Carmen, and it conveys a warning that if the singer decides to love someone, they should be very careful because love is a wild, untamable force.

La Habanera — The Habanera is a 19th-century Cuban musical and dance form with a distinctive rhythm that originated in Havana, from which it gets its name. It became popular worldwide and heavily influenced other musical genres, notably the Argentine tango and classical music, including the famous aria "Habanera" (L'amour est un oiseau rebelle) sung by the character Carmen in Georges Bizet's 1875 opera *Carmen*.

la toilette — the toilet

Votre toast, je peux vous le rendre — Your toast, I can give it back to you

These words are the words of the first line of the Toreador song in Bizet's 1875 opera Carmen.

Pastis — anise-flavored spirit of France

L'addition — the bill

Merci — Thank you

Cravate — tie

CHAPTER 9 — LA CORNUE

Merveilleux — marvelous

Quel four exceptionnel — What an exceptional oven

Vieil homme — old man

Voyez, je suis en bonne forme. Je retourne dans mon jardin. — See, I am in good shape. I am going back to my garden.

Oui, mais vous restez quand même humain. Vous avez besoin de manger et de boire de l'eau. Et de vous reposer! — Yes, but you are still human. You need to eat and drink. And rest!

CHAPTER 11 — THE VOICE IN MY HEAD

Au revoir, Le Chat — Goodbye, cat!

Courgette — zucchini

Aubergine — eggplant

Plat du jour — Plate of the day

Soupe d'aspèrges — asparagus soup

Poulet rôti au fenouil et riz à l'oignon — roast chicken with fennel and onion rice

Une petite salade verte — a small green salad

Nous devons changer le menu pour le dîner de demain — We need to change the menu for tomorrow's dinner

Chapter 12 — Crossroads

Tournesol — turn sun or sunflower

Espions, vous êtes des espions. Ce sont les Américains de la villa qui vous ont envoyé, n'est-ce pas ? Espions ! Espions ! Espions ! Espions ! — Spies ! You are spies! Did the Americans send you? Spies ! Spies ! Spies ! Spies !

Chapter 13 — Matching Problems to Their Solutions

Pastis — is an anise-flavored spirit and apéritif traditionally from France, typically containing less than 100 g/L sugar and 40–45% ABV

Ministère de la Culture, s'il te plaît. — Ministry of Culture, please.

Ministère de l'Agriculture — Ministry of Agriculture

Agneau — lamb

Chapter 14 — Nothing To Do and No One to Do It With

Bonjour, ami de Dave. — Good Day, friend of Dave.

Comment aimerais-tu commencer ta journée — How would you like to start your day?

poulet rôti — roast chicken

Chapter 15 — Foreigners

Qu'est-ce que c'est? — What is that?

Groseilles — gooseberries

Dinde — turkey

Grand-mère — grandmother

Papi and Mamie — grandpa and grandma

Boucher — butcher

La boucherie — the butcher shop

Chapter 16 — The Treasure

"Bonjour, Pomme, voici Daniel, l'un de nos invités. Il m'a aidé à charger les melons ce matin." — Good morning, Apple. This is Daniel, one of our guests. He helped me load the melons this morning.

"Son grand-père vivait à L'Esprit du Rhône quand il était petit et l'aidait à cueillir des melons." — His grandfather lived in L'Esprit du Rhône when he was a boy and helped pick melons.

"Oui, et il s'est perdu dans les bois." — Yes, and he got lost in the woods.

ganga cata — pin-tailed sandgrouse

Chapter 17 — The Legacy

Vignoble — vineyard

References

Chapter 2 — Second Act

Chateaux Neuf de Pape — https://en.wikipedia.org/wiki/
Ch%C3%A2teauneuf-du-Pape_AOC

Department of Vaucluse — https://es.wikipedia.org/wiki/Vaucluse

Chapter 3 — Affair with French Architecture

Garbure — https://www.simplefrenchcooking.com/recipe-entry/garbure

La Cornue — Le Château Range — https://lacornue.com/en-GB/chateau/
range-information

Chapter 7 — French Lessons

Mistral — https://en.wikipedia.org/wiki/Mistral_(wind)

Chapter 8 — The Habanera Effect

La Habanera — https://www.youtube.com/watch?v=KJ_HHRJf0xg

Theatre Antique d' Orange — https://en.wikipedia.org/wiki/Roman_
Theatre_of_Orange

Chapter 9 — Le Cornue

La Cornue — Le Château Range — https://lacornue.com/en-GB/chateau/
range-information

CHAPTER 10 — A LITTLE BIRD TOLD ME

Dentelles du Montmirail — https://en.wikipedia.org/wiki/Dentelles_de_Montmirail

Rock climbing, mountains — https://climb-europe.com/rockclimbingshop/rock-climbing-france-south-eastern-areas-map

Mount Ventoux — https://www.avignon-et-provence.com/en/natural-sites/mont-ventoux

Forteresse de Mornas — https://www.forteresse-mornas.fr/

Vichy Government — https://es.wikipedia.org/wiki/Francia_de_Vichy

Mignonne Line — https://en.wikipedia.org/wiki/Maginot_Line

CHAPTER 11 — CLAIRE

Avignon — https://es.wikipedia.org/wiki/Avi%C3%B1%C3%B3n

Paláis de Papas — https://en.wikipedia.org/wiki/Palais_des_Papes

Musee Calvet — https://en.wikipedia.org/wiki/Calvet_Museum

Nîmes Amphitheater — https://en.wikipedia.org/wiki/Arena_of_N%C3%AEmes

Sete — https://en.wikipedia.org/wiki/S%C3%A8te

CHAPTER 13 — MATCHING PROBLEMS TO SOLUTIONS

French Ministry of Culture — National Museum and Property Recovery — https://www.culture.gouv.fr/nous-connaitre/organisation-du-ministere/le-secretariat-general/mission-de-recherche-et-de-restitution-des-biens-culturels-spolies-entre-1933-et-1945/biens-musees-nationaux-recuperation-mnr#:~:text=R%C3%A9partition%20des%20MNR,sont%20donc%20pas%20tous%20restituables

Bastille Day — https://en.wikipedia.org/wiki/Bastille_Day

CHAPTER 14 — NOTHING TO DO AND NO ONE TO DO IT WITH

Bridge of Avignon — https://www.avignon-et-provence.com/en/monuments/bridge-avignon

Camp des Milles — https://en.wikipedia.org/wiki/Camp_des_Milles

Les Milles Film — Le Train De La Liberte — https://www.imdb.com/title/tt0110330/

Varian Fry — https://en.wikipedia.org/wiki/Varian_Fry

Righteous Among Nations — https://en.wikipedia.org/wiki/Righteous_Among_the_Nations

CHAPTER 15 — FOREIGNERS

Carites Austria — https://en.wikipedia.org/wiki/Caritas_Internationalis#:~:text=Emergency%20relief%20efforts%20and%20coordination,the%201967%20Arab%E2%80%93Israeli%20War.

The 1951 Refugee Convention — https://www.unhcr.org/about-unhcr/overview/1951-refugee-convention

Vienna's Role — While not the location of the convention›s signing, Vienna is a hub for migration and refugee-related activities, particularly through the ICMPD and the UNHCR office.

Resources

Savage Continent — https://en.wikipedia.org/wiki/Savage_Continent

The Survival of the Jews in France 1940-1944 — https://www.sciencespo.fr/research/cogito/home/the-survival-of-the-jews-in-france-1940-1944/?lang=en

Nîmes Committee — https://www.holocaustrescue.org/Nîmes-committee-leaders

Memorial Site of Les Milles Camp — https://www.campdesmilles.org/home2.html